SINGULAR STORIES

Tales from Singapore
Volume One

SINGULAR STORIES

Tales from Singapore
Volume One

**selected & with an introduction
by Robert Yeo**

Yang Publishers, Singapore
Three Continents Press, Washington, D.C.

Compilation and Introduction ©Robert Yeo 1993

Yang Publishers
44 Jalan Sembilang
Singapore 2057

ISBN 981-00-3939-5

Published in North America by:

Three Continents Press
1901 Pennsylvania Ave., N.W.
Suite 407
Washington, DC 20006   USA

Library of Congress Cataloging-in-Publication Data:

Singular stories : tales from Singapore / edited by Robert Yeo.
          p.   cm.
  Includes bibliographical references.
  ISBN 0-89410-757-7 (v. 1) — ISBN 0-89410-758-5 (pbk. : v. 1)
  1. Short stories, Singapore (English) 2. Singapore—Fiction.
I. Yeo, Robert.
PR9570.S52S55 1992
823'.010895957—dc20   92-34216
                                  CIP

Distributed in Singapore by Lim Swee Heng Trading Co.
42 Jalan Rabu; Singapore 2057; Tel: 4529290

Cover art by Max Winkler
©Three Continents Press 1993

Printed in Singapore by Book Press Pte. Ltd.

Table of Contents

Acknowledgements

The publishers would like to thank the editors of the journal *SINGA* for permission to reprint Kirpal Singh's "Monologue," Ho Poh Fun's "Rite of Passage," and Lim Thean Soo's "Sailboat."

The publishers would also like to thank Times Books International (Singapore) for permission to reprint Gopal Baratham's "Wedding Night," which was first published in the collection *Figments of Experience* (1981). Times Books also published Shirley Lim's *Another Country* (1982), where the story of the same title first appeared.

Ho Minfong's "Tanjong Rhu" and Ovidia Yu's "A Dream of China" both appear in *Prizewinning Asian Fiction*, edited by Leon Comber and published by Times Books International (1991). "Tanjong Rhu" has also been published in *Tanjong Rhu and Other Stories*, Federal Publications (Singapore), 1986. "A Dream of China" was first published in *Asiaweek* magazine, January 18, 1985.

"The Lady in Red" by Felix Chia was first published in his collection *The Lady in Red & Her Companions* by Heinemann in 1984. "Between the Lines" by Rebecca Chua was first published in her collection *The Newspaper Editor and Other Stories*, also by Heinemann, in 1981.

Woo Keng Thye's "Out of the Storm" first appeared in *A Question of Time*, published by Sam Boyd Enterprise in 1983.

A Note on the Selection

The stories here were written or published during the period 1980-1984. They are chosen from individual collections and magazines, and include two stories which have won first prize in the annual *Asiaweek* short story competition, namely "Tanjong Rhu" by Ho Minfong and "A Dream of China" by Ovidia Yu.

I am not able to obtain permission to use the story "The Landlord" by Wong Swee Hoon and very much regret its exclusion.

Robert Yeo

Introduction[1]

Robert Yeo

Catherine Lim declared, in a revealing 1983 interview, "But I'm definitely interested in people."

This remark could very likely be used as a credo for her writing and for much of short story writing in Singapore, to point to the fact that most Singaporean writers are realists, interested in people, interested in portraying people directly in actual, verifiable contexts.

This point is emphasized if comparison is made with the stories of Gabriel García Márquez. The magical realism of the stories in *Innocent Erendira and Other Stories* cannot be successfully judged by the criteria applied to naturalistic fiction. Except for "Death Beyond Constant Love," whose reading yields a meaning in terms of plot, character, and suggestion in the setting of a poor third world country, the rest of the stories defy the attempt at realistic interpretation. Some of them are almost abstract prose poems, in which Márquez' major preoccupation appears to be the dream lives of his characters. They are caught in situations often nightmarish and their actions and speech are dream-like and repetitious. What action there is is cyclical and often subordinated to the recurrence of images and symbols the nature of which can be gathered by reference to the cryptic titles of the stories: "The Sea of Lost Time," "Eva is Inside the Cat," "Dialogue with the Mirror," and "Eyes of a Blue Dog."

---

[1]This essay first appeared as "The Singapore Short Story," in *Tenggara* 26 (1990), 114-119. It has been slightly revised, and the bibliography added, for the purposes of this publication.

The result is a blend of form and content that is unique and reminds one of the films of another South American artist, the surrealist master Luis Bunuel. The experience of reading these stories is often one of confusion, if one searches for meaning that could be summed up logically. It seems best to surrender oneself to being in a state of unknowing, of responding to the linguistic word play and succession of images and symbols, and let the experience remain sensuous and indefinable.

Adherence to realism can be a trap leading to a piling of facts not integral to the story. Quite of a few of the stories of Singaporeans Lim Thean Soo, Woo Keng Thye, and Wong Swee Hoon drag under the weight of excessive documentation which, the writers feel, is necessary to establish the background.

The large majority of Singaporean stories conforms to traditional structure, with distinct beginnings, middles, and ends; this structure could also incorporate the surprise ending. For Lim, as he says in the Preface to his collection *Blues and Carnation* (1985), "my emphasis is always on the storyline." Earlier on, in the Preface to *The Parting Gift & Other Stories*, he writes: "The story's brevity dictates that it must absorb the readers' interest from the beginning to the end using well-known ploys such as the twist at the end, the onslaught of surprise after surprise, and the sort of dénouement that just stops short of a complete explanation."

This describes accurately most of the stories written by Singaporeans in the 1980s. Through the Prefaces to his books and through other essays, Lim has provided information about his practice; Catherine Lim, too, in interviews, has revealed her approach to the short story. But apart from them, other writers have not elaborated on their technique. Elsewhere, in an article "Catherine Lim and the Singapore Short Story" (1981), I have tried to show how well Lim understands and accepts the main features of the well-structured tale with its emphasis on story and suspense leading to foreseen or unforeseen ends. In addition, the point of view evident in her first book, significantly entitled *Little Ironies*, is sustained in later books; in fact, the ironic orientation she has given to the form is part of her distinct contribution to the short story. Irony is there from the beginning: notably in "The Teacher" from *Little Ironies* (1978), "Or Else, The Lightning God" from *Or Else, The Lightning God and Other Stories* (1980), "Lee Geok Chan" from *They Do Return* (1983), and

2

"The English Language Teacher's Secret" from *The Shadow of a Shadow of a Dream* (1987). The irony is also not absent in her later collection, *O Singapore! Stories in Celebration* (1989), but this book is otherwise a departure for Lim and will be discussed in more detail below.

Though she is technically skilled, Rebecca Chua has received little critical attention. Her book *The Newspaper Editor and Other Stories* (1981) contains stories about people in their twenties caught in personal stagnation with glimpses of better lives unrealised. Her stories often unfold in quick cuts reminiscent of the cinema and in this sense she is experimental, differing from the majority of Singaporean story-tellers. "Suicide" and "Vortices" are good examples of her technique, while "Between the Lines" demonstrates how cleverly though self-consciously this technique works.

Gopal Baratham is an ironist and his satire ranges from the tolerant to the biting. His "Wedding Night" reveals a cool style that exposes as coarse the open, unsophisticated Tamil attitude toward sexual and other misdemeanours. "Gretchen's Choice," from his second collection *People Make You Cry*, cuts away the cream of Western manners in which Gretchen is layered and uncovers a naïve girl unable to resist the shameful emotional blackmail of her traditional Tamil father.

Although the dominant mode of Singaporean writing is naturalistic, all the stories in Catherine Lim's recent collection *O Singapore! Stories in Celebration* are departures from this standard. In the context of her own writing, these stories move away significantly from the earlier works that mirror reality. Lim's writing had thus far progressed to encompass grittier subject matter, such as working-class themes (prostitution and vagrancy) and bold topics (transvestism in "Father and Son"), and to lengthen and flesh out the plots (particularly in *The Shadow of a Shadow of a Dream*) beyond the "single incident" concept. Nonetheless, these earlier stories remain naturalistic, portraying ordinary people who behave credibly and predictably in a known social context.

But in *O Singapore!*, while the social context is recognisable (Singapore in the 1980s), the ordinary people are seen to behave in extraordinary ways. Take, for example, "The Malady and the Cure": the "faceless" civil servant, after years of faithful adherence and indeed pandering to public campaigns which exhort him and other

3

Singaporeans not to spit, not to litter, etc., becomes a victim of a painful malady that makes it impossible for him to discharge his duties and obligations as a good government employee. His doctor diagnoses the problem as one caused by a too-strict observance of the injunctions of public campaigns and prescribes a cure that urges him not only to violate the injunctions but also to do other acts of discourtesy. It is soon discovered that other civil servants are similarly afflicted and a large-scale remedy must be devised: in neighbouring Johor (Malaysia), in cooperation with their state government, a special plot of land is put aside to allow the ailing Singaporean civil servants to perpetuate acts of extreme rudeness not allowed or publicly frowned upon at home.

Lim's deliberate deviation from naturalism assumes forms that recall the behaviour of characters in the plays of Shakespeare and Ben Jonson who fall under the influence of a "humour." Such persons display psychological traits of paranoid proportions and behave in ways which are exaggerated and extreme, designed to stretch and violate credibility. In addition to such characterization, one notices too that Lim is less interested in crafting a well-made short story with its familiar fine-tuned plot, in favour of the incredible and the unpredictable. The forms of her stories have changed too: "Kiasuism: A Socio-Historico-Cultural Perspective" is written like a pedantic academic paper; "In Search of (A Play)" is cast like a play; and "Write, Right, Rite: or 'How Catherine Lim Tries to Offer Only the Best on the Altar of Good Singapore Writing'" proceeds through a series of exchanges of letters between the Catherine Lim persona and various public institutions. Fantasy, not present in Lim's previous stories, becomes dominant in this collection; Koh Tai Ann is correct in describing the stories as "fantasies" in her review of O Singapore! (The Straits Times, 7 June 1989).

Style alters, from story to story, to cope with Lim's pursuit of the fantastic. "In Search of (A Play)" presents the Confucian sage speaking in a manner that parodies English translations of the Analects of Confucius ("Yes, the master he say virtuous woman always must prepare to copulate with man.").

In form and style, Catherine Lim's O Singapore! introduces the Singaporean short story in experimental flow. Rebecca Chua's cutting technique has been mentioned. Likewise, Kirpal Singh's "Little Sister Writes Home," in which an entire story is written in a register of

4

Singapore English (or "Singlish"), is reminiscent of Catherine Lim's earlier "The Taximan's Story"; Singh, as Lim before him, skilfully exploits the idiomatic richness of "Singlish," and one must hope for more experimentation in this direction in fiction. This has already been done with considerable success in stage plays, especially in S. Kon's astonishing monologue *Emily of Emerald Hill*. The popular and critical success of this play points to the possibilities of the repertoire of "Singlish" as a magical medium for speech and narrative. In the case of *Emily*, there is more speech than narration, and it is up to writers of fiction, whether in the short story or the novel, to show what can be done with narration. It is quite possible that one will write a novel that will match the Singapore English of *Emily*, and become for Singaporean fiction what *The Adventures of Huckleberry Finn* is for American fiction.

"There are so many different kinds of short story that the genre as a whole seems constantly to resist universal definition . . ." writes Valerie Shaw in her Preface to *The Short Story: A Critical Introduction* (1983). Shaw takes as her scope the international short story and discusses modern masters who write in English such as Henry James, James Joyce, Katherine Mansfield, and Elizabeth Bowen, as well as those who do not use English such as Franz Kafka and Jorge Luis Borges. Stories written in English in Singapore obviously do not have the variety of form and theme found internationally; this point has already been made in my discussion of the short fiction of Márquez. There is no indication that any Singaporean writers have been influenced by or have benefitted from their reading of innovators like Kafka and Borges, assuming that they've read the stories of either of these writers.

Very little is known, in fact, about the reading habits of Singaporean writers of short fiction and the extent to which they are influenced by the genre as it has evolved and is now practised worldwide. Judging by the stories, it is safe to conclude that Singaporean writers prefer the relative safety of naturalism or realism and have learned to construct the short story in terms of a well-defined, single-moment plot, clear characterization, and a resolute or indeterminate end. There are few innovative tales featuring the surrealism of Kafka, the magical realism of Márquez, or the labyrinthine mazes of Borges; these writers have responded to the urgings of their personal visions of the worlds they inhabit and make, and in the

5

process have transformed the short story into almost unrecognisable moulds. (A notable Singaporean exception is Gregory Nalpon, who has regretfully left only a small body of mostly unpublished work.) Nevertheless, to judge by the sheer output, stamina, and quality of writers such as Catherine Lim, Lim Thean Soo, and Goh Sin Tub, the 1980s belong to the short story writers, just as the 1960s and 1970s belonged to the poets.[2] Philip Jeyaratnam's *First Loves* and Lim's *O Singapore!* not only made it to the Times Bookshops bestseller lists but stayed there for months, and Jeyaratnam's book topped the list. In doing so, their books earned for Singaporean fiction a mass readership and this is likely to secure for short fiction a ready audience, provided the authors can continue to deliver. Delivery, of course, depends also on how discriminating readers are: the bestselling success of the hastily assembled *True Singapore Ghost Stories* in 1989 points to the thirst of readers for supernatural sensationalism no matter how badly written. However, the success of two books as varied as *First Loves* (which consists of a series of linked stories and a section of three different stories) and *O Singapore!* (which consists of non-realistic deviations from narration) reveals a more selective readership appreciative of the diversity of good short fiction.

It is also significant that Singaporean writers have recently won top prizes in the annual *Asiaweek* short story competition, which invites writers from throughout Southeast and East Asia. Ho Minfong began when she won first prize in the 1982 competition with her entry "Tanjong Rhu"; Ovidia Yu continued, also winning first prize in the 1984 competition with "A Dream of China"; and in 1986 Nalla Tan took second prize with "What You Asked." This is indicative, surely, of merit beyond national recognition.

These achievements in Singaporean short fiction in the 1980s translate into Singaporean sales in excess of 10,000 copies (a large number for a country of only 2.7 million), and the gradual replacement of Western writers with local writers on the bookshelves and in the review columns. The Times Bookstores Bestseller list of 31 December 1989 presents four Singaporeans in the top six spots:

---

[2]The 1980s also saw the English-language theatre acquiring its national identity. Theatre is outside the scope of this essay but is necessarily part of the total picture.

6

3. *The Teenage Workbook* by Adrian Tan
4. *Miss Moorthy Investigates* by Ovidia Yu
5. *The Teenage Textbook* by Adrian Tan
6. *O Singapore!* by Catherine Lim

This points to a significant trend, which is the gradual but perceptible rise of mass Singaporean readership for home-grown authors. This trend is important not only sociologically but also artistically because, if the Singaporean writer is aware that he or she can appeal to a large number of local readers, then he or she may tend to write more for them. This is likely to have an artistic effect on what works are composed, and how they are composed.

Bibliography of Works Cited

Baratham, Gopal. *People Make You Cry*. Singapore: Times Books International, 1988.
_____. "Wedding Night." In *Figments of Experience*. Singapore: Times Books International, 1981.
Chua, Rebecca. *The Newspaper Editor and Other Stories*. Singapore: Heinemann, 1981.
Ho Minfong. "Tanjong Rhu." In *Tanjong Rhu and Other Stories*. Singapore: Federal Publications, 1986.
Jeyaratnam, Philip. *First Loves*. Singapore: Times Books International, 1987.
Kon, S. *Emily of Emerald Hill*. Singapore: Macmillan, 1989.
Lee, Russell, *et al*. *True Singapore Ghost Stories*. Singapore: Orchard Books, 1989.
Lim, Catherine. Interview, *Clout* (Singapore), April 1983, 33.
_____. *Little Ironies: Stories of Singapore*. Singapore: Heinemann, 1978.
_____. *O Singapore! Stories in Celebration*. Singapore: Times Books International, 1989.
_____. *Or Else, The Lightning God and Other Stories*. Singapore: Heinemann, 1980.
_____. *The Shadow of a Shadow of a Dream*. Singapore: Heinemann, 1987.

_____. *They Do Return*. Singapore: Times Books International, 1983.

Lim Thean Soo. *Blues and Carnation*. Singapore: Federal Publications, 1985.

_____. *The Parting Gift and Other Stories*. Singapore: Sri Keseva, 1981.

Márquez, Gabriel García. *Innocent Erendira and Other Stories*. Translated by Gregory Rabassa. New York: Harper & Row, 1978.

Shaw, Valerie. *The Short Story: A Critical Introduction*. Harlow, Essex: Longman, 1983.

Singh, Kirpal. "Little Sister Writes Home." In Platt, Ho, & Weber, eds., *Varieties of English Around the World: Singapore & Malaysia*. John Benjamin, 1983, pp. 134-136.

Tan, Adrian. *The Teenage Textbook*. Singapore: Landmark Books, 1988.

_____. *The Teenage Workbook*. Singapore: Landmark Books, 1989.

Tan, Nalla. "What You Asked." In *Hearts and Crosses*. Singapore: Heinemann, 1989.

Yeo, Robert. "Catherine Lim and the Singapore Short Story." In *Commentary* (Singapore), 5, 2 (1982), 38-47.

Yu, Ovidia. "A Dream of China." *Asiaweek*, January 18, 1985.

_____. *Miss Moorthy Investigates*. Singapore: Times Books International, 1989.

A Girl as Sweet as Alice

Gregory Nalpon

It must be remembered that Donatello Varga's father had once told him, "Listen you li'l rascal—choose the sweetest star in the sky and stand under it every night. Make a hollow with your palms and wait under the star and long for it and say good things to it. Ha! You know something? That sweet star is going to stay right where it is! Up there in the sky! But if you stand under it long enough, you will find in the cup of your palms a li'l pool of starlight. So boy, don't forget that!"

He stayed with his mother in Newton. They rented a room there. Donatello's father had died five years ago and Donatello was nineteen years of age.

He had two ambitions in life. One was to be admired by the whole world just as Fabian was. The other was to be a great trombonist like J. J. Johnson.

No one admired Donatello, except little boys to whom he would boast, so that listening, you would imagine that he was the most daring of men and the greatest lover since Casanova. Actually he had never fought anyone in his life and the presence of a pretty girl would reduce him to a state of speechless embarrassment.

Donatello was happy whenever a rich Chinese died. He'd play his father's trombone at the funeral for six dollars, followed by a scrumptious dinner and two large, cold bottles of beer. It was a good price for the wheezing bray his trombone would produce every time he tried to blow like J. J. Johnson.

Donatello appeared taller than he actually was on account of the wads of cardboard he stuffed into his shoes. He was quite pleasant to look at, if you could disregard his missing front teeth and the thick grease in his hair, which melted as soon as he walked into the sun, oiling his forehead and ears. He talked as he imagined Fabian would talk and walked with an exaggerated swagger. He collected empty packets of an expensive brand of cigarettes and filled them up with cheap cigarettes, so that everyone could see a packet of high-class cigarettes in the pocket of his transparent terylene shirt and also a crisp one-dollar note which he never spent. He wore a gold-tinted bracelet with his name embossed on it: Donatello Fabian Varga. A photograph of Brigitte Bardot, in her most kittenish pose, peered out of the cellophane window of his wallet. He'd flash it carelessly in crowded places and smile, quietly acknowledging the admiration he thought he detected in everyone's eyes.

He combed his hair whenever he found a mirror. He'd raise an eyebrow and shape a leer with his lips, and gazing at his reflection would say to himself, "Huh! You handsome hunk of a man, you!" He practised kissing for ten minutes every morning, on his pillow, in readiness for the day when he would devastate lovely women with his kisses.

Donatello had three friends: Harun, the headman of a gang in the area whom he ran errands for; Albert, a final-year seminarian; and Dai Kee, the conductor of the Chinese funeral band. For some reason, nobody else, apart from his mother and small boys, tolerated Donatello Varga.

One day, as he was relating fabulous exploits which he had thought up the night before to a group of small boys, one of them said, "My brother told me you are a big bluff! He said you're a lousy, stupid bluffer!"

Donatello was deeply hurt. "Go and tell your brother," he said sternly to the small boy, "that I'll bash him up! Man, I'll beat his brains out! Tell all your brothers that!"

He delivered this challenge exactly as Fabian would have done it. Then he turned on his heels and slouched away, feeling sad that the small boys had lost faith in him and also feeling afraid that their elder brothers might accept his challenge to fight.

He had seventeen dollars in his pocket at the time. He was saving money for a lilac-coloured Dacron suit and a blood-red silk shirt. But having lost his admirers and facing the prospect of a number of severe beatings, Donatello discarded the idea of the lilac suit and the blood-red shirt. He felt like investing in a couple of gallons of ice-cold beer. He couldn't go to any of the bars nearby. Word of his challenge may have already spread. He took a bus to Robinson Road, to the Midnight Bar and Restaurant.

It was a cool dim place with soft cushioned seats and tropical fish in aquariums, green fronds in corners, and lights like coloured berries on the ceiling.

When Donatello's eyes became accustomed to the light he chose a seat and sank into its softness. There were only a few customers in the bar. It was still early in the day. The waitresses sat together, chatting gaily. One of them, noticing Donatello, left the group and hurried to his table. She leaned over his table and looked at him in anticipation.

"A large beer," he said. And he became himself again: Donatello Fabian Varga, hero supreme, lady killer, debonair man of the world. Oh, she was a lovely thing, this girl. She was fair and shaped like some fragile statuette from Bali. Her lips were red and wet and smiling, her eyes large and shiny, her hair a careless wraith of smoke stroked gently over her ears. She wore a *kebaya* of black lace, which clung to her body and tiny waist, and a red sarong, pleated so that one smooth ankle was visible as she walked on gold-coloured high-heeled slippers to the bar to fill his order.

Donatello wondered whether what his father had told him could be applied in some way toward the conquest of this girl. He rehearsed what he'd say to her as soon as she brought the beer. He thought of leering at her and saying, "You got anything in mind for tonight, baby?" No, that wasn't good enough. How about, "Hi, honey, I've got plans for just you and me tonight! Let's go out and have a ball, oh, you cute chick, you!"

The girl came back with his beer before Donatello could make up his mind. She sat next to him. She placed a glass on a beer mat in front of him and filled it from a large cold bottle. She smiled at Donatello. He blushed and lowered his head. He couldn't think of anything to say. His heart thudded in his chest, so violently that he was sure his shirt fluttered to its rhythm. She edged closer to him. Donatello took a gulp of beer and choked. The girl stroked his back soothingly with her cool hand. Donatello could feel her long red fingernails on the skin of his back. He could feel the sudden rise of hundreds of goose pimples.

He muttered a protest. "Why, handsome, don't you like it?" she

11

asked softly. Donatello jerked away nervously and squeezed himself against the wall. The girl laughed, "Are you really scared of me? A big man like you?"

Donatello wished again that he could remember all the things he had rehearsed for just this kind of situation. The girl edged closer to him, and the goose pimples rose on his flesh.

"What's your name, handsome?" she whispered. Her eyes seemed to sparkle with little lights. Donatello blushed. He tried to answer her but the words stuck to his throat. He took a large swallow of beer. This time he didn't choke. He braced himself for the effort and stammered out, "D-d-d-donatello."

Her smile widened and her eyes softened. "That's a beautiful name," she said dreamily. "You know, some boys call themselves Ricky or Fabian, or Elvis or Cliff. They're ugly names. But your name, Don-a-tello, it's just like music."

Donatello immediately decided to drop the Fabian part of his name. It wasn't his real name anyway. He had borrowed it. He took another great gulp of beer. "What's your name?" he asked.

"Oh, it's not as nice as your name. My name's Alice." Her name fell on Donatello's ears with a sound sweeter than a chorus of porcelain bells. Alice filled his empty glass. "Another beer?" she asked. He nodded.

"Alright, sweetheart, I'll be right back," she said. She smiled at him, blinked with wide eyes playfully, and hurried away. Donatello's heart shivered in a frenzy of emotion. He felt a tremendous desire to do something great and noble for Alice.

"You know, you're a very nice boy," Alice said after she had brought a new bottle of beer and filled his glass and sat so close to him that he could smell the scent of her soft black hair. "I don't think you can help being a nice boy with a name like yours," she said.

"I'm not a boy," Donatello said, more confident now of himself. "I'm nineteen."

Alice laughed gaily. "All right, old man, I'm eighteen, unmarried, and very, very lonely for a handsome devil like you."

"You, you mean you're not married?" Donatello stammered. "Doesn't anyone love you?"

Alice pouted her wet, red lips at him and blinked her eyes naughtily. "Don't you have any boyfriends?" Donatello demanded.

"Oh, millions of them," she said, "and all of them swear that they love me."

"Then why don't you get married?" Donatello asked.

"Not a single dog in the pack wants to marry me," she said. "Do you want to marry me, sweetheart?"

Donatello did not believe her. What she just said couldn't be possible. But there came to him the realisation of a great and noble thing he would do for her. He would get her a husband. That's what he would do! He would find a good man to marry her so that she'd grow plump and happy and have many children.

"I'll get you a husband," he blurted out. "Would you like that?"

"Oh, you're sweet," she said, smiling at him for a moment and tightening her fingers over his. He drew ten dollars from his wallet and handed it to her. "I must go now," he said. "Keep the change."

Donatello stood up and Alice allowed him enough space to squeeze past her. "I'll be back this evening," he said. "I'll bring a husband for you."

"Goodbye, Donatello," Alice called after him. Anyone who looked closely at her would have detected a mistiness in her eyes.

Donatello walked out of the Midnight Bar and Restaurant. He strode like a man. He had quite forgotten his usual swagger. He was not aware of the ten dollar note which Alice had slipped into his back pocket as he had squeezed past her. Donatello was filled with resolve and determination. He was going to get a husband for Alice.

He took a bus back to Newton. He remembered that he might have to face a number of scuffles. But strangely, the thought didn't bother him. He could think only of a husband for Alice. There were three choices: Arun, the gangleader; Albert, the seminarian; and Dai Kee, the conductor of the Chinese funeral band.

He went to see Harun first. "Nothing you can do for me today," Harun said tersely. "Get lost!" Donatello took the hint. Anyway, a man like that couldn't be good enough for Alice.

Albert was at home on holiday. When Donatello asked him whether he wanted a lovely girl to be his wife, Albert patted him good-naturedly on the back and gave him a short sermon on the beauty of celibacy.

And Bai Kee was no good either. He had three wives already, he said, and he had neither the money nor the inclination for a fourth. As it was, three wives created enough hell for one man. "In fact," he told Donatello, "I wish I had never married at all."

Donatello Varga was a desperate man by now. There wasn't anyone else he could ask. He didn't know anyone else. He collected his trombone from Bai Kee and walked all the way to the waterfront. He played low mournful notes on the trombone, thinking deeply all the while. Even a tugboat's grunted answer to the trombone didn't draw a response from him. He wondered how he could apply his father's talk about pools of starlight to his current situation.

Night fell on the waterfront and Donatello Varga roused enough courage to do what he had to do. He entered the Midnight Bar and Restaurant cradling the trombone under his arm. Alice spotted him immediately and sat down at his table.

"Hello," she said. "I expected you earlier."

"I was busy," Donatello said.

"Oh, you poor dear," she crooned, stroking his arm. "Did you bring that trombone to serenade me tonight?"

"Alice . . ." Donatello said, and then he found that he couldn't say what he had resolved he would say. Alice saw his difficulty.

"I'll get you a beer," she murmured and hurried to the bar. Donatello felt very ashamed and afraid. Ashamed because he had not kept his promise to her and afraid because he was obliged to make compensation which might not please her.

Alice came back with the beer, filled his glass, and sat close to him. "What's worrying you, sweetheart?" she whispered. She looked so cool and so lovely that he had to swallow the tightness in his throat. He looked away.

"I haven't brought you a husband," he muttered. Alice was silent. Oh, the poor thing, she thought, he really meant what he said. He really meant it . . .

"That's okay!" she said after a while.

Donatello made an effort to control his nervousness. "Will you marry me," he stammered.

Alice closed her hand over his. Her lips parted slightly and her eyes grew wet. "Of course, you idiot," she said huskily. "Didn't I ask you in the first place?"

Late that night, the elder brothers of the small boys went out to look for Donatello in answer to his challenge. They finally found him sitting by the waterfront. Alice lay snuggled lovingly against his shoulders as he blew low, peaceful notes on his trombone.

Donatello and Alice looked so happy that the boys decided to leave them alone. Somehow they respected Donatello from that day on. Any man who could get a girl as sweet as Alice deserved respect.

Between the Lines

Rebecca Chua

his name is whitney

Airports frighten me. They are cold and bright with lights and insinuating, throaty voices that metallise over microphones. The ground echoes with racing trolleys and thundering footsteps of rushing, faceless masses, people who push, and porters who weave in and out of columns and children and coats.

he was a strange boy   beautiful straight soft hair

I stand with my suitcases colliding at my feet, with movement churning all around me, with lights reflecting in my glazed eyes, the constant eddy of distant voices that grow louder as they approach, then diminish as they turn corners, vanish down the corridors.

limpid eyes   that were golden black   almost too black   such
hidden depths   for a boy of eleven   almost

In the airport toilet the faucets are tight and rusty and only a trickle of russet water splashes on my out-stretched palm. Rows and rows of grubby green doors are reflected eight times in the rectangular mirrors that hang above the eight sinks standing in rank.

he was tall for eleven   tall for Chinese   they all said a boy
with a thin sallow face   a determined chin   like his father's
high cheekbones   a Mandarin

17

My eyes are large in the mirror that hangs askew over the stained, cracked sink, eyes that are bloodshot with having had too much to drink and too little weeping. My face is blurred and blotchy, the outline indeterminate, the full cheeks patched with blusher, the mouth too red.

he always wore the black velvet coat that was too big for him
his father's coat he said   or liked to pretend but he had never
seen his father   who had left him when he was still an
embryo

Beyond the tarmac, dusk mists the water-colour grey skies. The winds whistlewhip through the hangars, penetrate the bones of brittle grey buildings. Mottled ash shrouds the greying green shrubs. Trees are dirt-damascened, gnarled, as if burned skeletons whose finger-like branches point downward to a ground, not brown, that receives dust to dust, ashes to ashes.

he had such a serious face   one hardly remembered his smile
at first   it was perhaps   as if   he was too polite   "you first"
he seemed to intimate   though it always remained unspoken
"you first"   his head cocked   his eyes guarded   impenetrable

There are no roads. I see only the vast grey darkness. And that is indistinguishable from the vast grey sky. The roads are dark except for pinpoints of fireflies that hover on the banks of the muddy grey-blue riverine roads, ash-grey streams that stop, or slouch outward, directionless.

he was a solemn little boy   he remained apart   uncommuni-
cative   his eyes comprehending   but not saying a word   he
would look out the window as if contemplating another
world   another time

We go through the routine checks. Deft hands that feel our bodies under our clothes, geigers that crackle protestingly as they sweep from top to toe. I surrender my handbag for inspection, submit to the safety precautions like a dutiful passenger should. I walk through the scanner and make for the departure exit.

on cold nights he huddled under thin blankets and shivered
the tears he struggled with alone   knelt in the moonlight to
pray   because he had been taught   but not really believing
the ritual   this God to whom his prayers were addressed
whom he had never seen   just like his father   was God like
his father?

The cabin is compact, claustrophobic, low-ceilinged. It is a pressurised cocoon, rocking gently, inconspicuously, reassuringly. It is warm with lights and upholstery and the smiles of the cabin crew. It rustles with voices and music and the clinking of glasses, the carpet-cushioned muffled sounds of stiletto heels.

he was curiously self-sufficient, already, at eleven   well
almost   he was gentle, polite, unresisting, preoccupied with
his own thoughts   he often sat quietly   by the window
carelessly tracing patterns on the window pane   as the rain
sloshed down on the other side

I can see the wing from my window, the spurt of flame as the engines rev and the plane is propelled forward. The blast of noise, bursting in my eardrums, crescendos. I look out the window. The buildings are dark squares of enclosed light in boxed panes blazing without heat, without passion. But unremitting, perennial. The airport will always look like this. Next month, next year.

the other children in the class responded   but he was indiffer-
ent   though she ached to love him   she saw him as a
changeling   misunderstood   he remained indifferent to her
entreaties, her biscuits, her attempts at gaining his interest
though she bought him story books, coloured pencils, toy
trains, mechanical cars   he played with them for a while
then went to sit by the window, quietly looking out

The plane traverses the runway, up, down and around, twice, thrice, a fourth time, following a path charted by the control tower. It is radar-monitored, everything minutely synchronised, even as other planes whir and screech on the runway, coming in, or about to take off. It is all a matter of timing, split-second precision.

was he looking out for his father?   waiting for him to come
back?   she could not draw him away from the window
though she tried   and she cried   because she thought she had
failed him as a teacher

The plane points its nose to the sky, rights itself, cruises. Now
the blast is no longer a roar. It is a hum in my ear, soothing, a
continuous drowsydrone.

he haunted her   this little orphan boy   made her feel guilty
frustrated   because she could not seem to reach him   he was
self-sufficient in his own little eleven-year-old world   and she
felt shut out   ignored   ignominious

There are clouds outside my window, soft and diaphanous,
draped in a sea of blue-like boa feathers. The sky is water-colour
blue, like waves. Already it is morning. It is another day.

he brought a dog to school one day   it was a yellow mongrel
who fought with other mongrels in the city streets and had
survived   it was always laughing   always panting   its
tongue hanging out to one side   its teeth glistening   white
with saliva   its tail wagging

The gentleman in the next seat is snoring quietly into his lapel,
his beard brushing his shirt-collar rhythmically.

he would pat the dog often   but absently   as if on second
thought   although the dog followed him everywhere   at first
she was angry   she said the dog disrupted her lessons   she
insisted he put it out into the street where it belonged

The stewardess brings me a tray of orange juice, a cold roll, foil-
wrapped butter and jam, a croissant, a cake, plastic cutlery, plastic
cups and saucers. The gentleman in the next seat wakes up.

"David!" she cried "I will not have a dog in the class!"   he
looked at her, surprised   for a minute he did not move then
he motioned to the dog who followed him out of the class

20

I take a book out to read. That will distract me for two more hours, perhaps. Actually, I have already begun reading the book, but I cannot remember where I paused, so I start again. After a while, I find myself reading the same line in the same paragraph again and again. I recognise the words, but not the sense.

she resumed the lesson as if there had been no interruption
but he did not return   she kept pausing to look at the door
as if she could will him to return   finally she couldn't stand
it anymore   she sent another little boy to look for him   but
he did not return either

The plane is cruising, coasting the islands of white clouds, now fluffier in a glaring white sky that reflects light like aluminium. The wing gleams unbearably. I pull down the shutter and there is immediately a pall.

in fear and anticipation and desperation   she told the class
to continue reading   while she went out in search of David
her heels striking the linoleum that paved the corridor

I push up the shutter but the sun scorches, sears, and I automatically pull it down again. The flight stewardess passes by on her rounds, concern in her smile. Is everything alright? Yes. I go back to my book.

she opened the door at the end of the corridor that led out
into the courtyard   the scorching sunlight made her blink
David was standing in his black velvet coat that was too big
for him   tears trickling down his face   the mongrel had
been struck down   and lay whimpering

The book is not good enough. The journey is too long drawn-out. Suddenly regret stings my nostrils, nostalgia aches in my stomach, just underneath the ribs. Suddenly I want very badly not to have left, not to be going home to a place I have not seen, nor called home, for six years. But already it is too late.

21

"David!" she whispered, shocked   he looked up at her   his face pale   his eyes limpid   large   she could see what he was thinking   he knew what she was thinking   he looked down lovingly, regretfully at the mongrel, shook his head

Maybe, I think, I should not have gone.

she moved toward him   he stood still   but she saw the apprehension in his eyes   though he did not flinch, she saw his face blanch, his pupils dilate as if she had hit him   suddenly his shoulders were shaking   she was wide-eyed   nonplussed   she knelt, took him in her arms   felt his instinctive hardening   and then he had broken away from her and was running

But, then, everyone was going to London. And I wanted to, too.

she wanted to call him   stop him   she was afraid he might come to harm   but there was nothing she could do   she picked up the mongrel, cradling it in her arms, and took it indoors

My mother will be waiting at the airport, an anxious, fluttering hen. She will bring with her my father, who would have preferred to sit at home and watch TV; my brother, who would complain that he had had to give away his prized seats to the football match at the National Stadium just to be dragged along to welcome me home; and a whole gaggle of relatives.

she nursed the mongrel   used the cylindrical rubber-capped tube from a bottle of eyedrops to squirt milk down its throat   it whimpered still   its eyes large and limpid and trapped

My mother will be full of questions. She will want to know how the flight was, why I look so thin. She is convinced I starve myself in London, where there is no one to cook for me (meaning herself). Worst of all, she will want to know everything. Everything within two minutes of my arrival. She will chastise me for being tongue-tied. But I do not know what to say in an airport full of people.

> *David stayed away from school for two days   she was worried he might be sick   she looked up his address in the school register   set out one afternoon   found him sitting on the top step of a mouldy tenement building, looking idly at passing cars and passers-by   "David," she said   he looked at her blankly   he said, and it was as if each word was a stone aimed at her, "I don't have a dog"   "Not any more," he said and then, "He's dead, isn't he?"   "No, David, no," she tried to explain   "I hit him," he said, as if that was the end of it she shook her head, trying   "Please go away" he said wearily, "you didn't want him anymore"   it hit her then guilt   guilt flooded her vision   "I'm sorry," she said inadequately   "Will you come home with me?"   "I don't want him anymore," he said   "Will you come back to school then?" she asked   "Okay" just one word   already he had turned his back on her*

I push up the shutter. The clouds are scudding in an orange sky. Down below, the patches of green fields and clumps of orchards give way to long tall white boxes in a concrete jungle that stretches for acres. The captain's suave voice crackles over the microphone. We are going to stop for refuelling. The lights flicker red. Fasten your seat-belts. No smoking. I obey.

> *he was back in the classroom early the next morning in the black velvet coat that was too big for him   the dog was there wagging his tail   David ignored him   watching him, she despaired   he looked at her, wide-eyed, distant   "But I don't want him anymore," he echoed   the dog went up to him, licked his hand experimentally   David stood motionless, his hand hanging down   she held her breath slowly, reluctantly, he patted the dog, bent one ear, fondled it   its tail wagged hard   its tongue all over his hand   David bent down on one knee, struggling to right his heavy coat   suddenly he had buried his head in the furry neck of the dog   "Oh, David," she whispered, "I'm so sorry" and her cheek was glistening with a single escaped tear*

The plane is descending from level to level, not quite bumping. But I can feel it. It is going too fast. The pressure is rushing into my ears, into my head. I see the seat in front flying to meet my head. Nausea grips me in the throat, sticks in my esophagus. I take a deep breath. Several breaths. I shut my eyes.

he was pale   his eyes large and limpid   his cheek bones stood out   his mouth vulnerable   and still she did not recognise the signs   he was thin,   no, thinner   but then, he had always been thin and the black velvet coat enveloped him   it was still negligence   she would always blame herself

When I open my eyes, the plane is coming to a halt along the runway. They throw the doors open. I alight dutifully, walk with the other passengers into a transit lounge which is crowded and stuffy. I sit in a corner, watching a couple of tourists asking the price of a gaudy plastic souvenir.

after so many months, it was too late   the doctor said he had to be hospitalised for tests, treatment   she should have known, she told herself   whitney found her in hysterics, found the dog   bewildered "don't, please don't" he begged but she could not stop crying   though the doctor had exonerated her   "he's going to die," she cried, "just like the dog"   whitney didn't know what she was talking about   "I didn't want him there"   guilt came flooding back   it had been a childish retaliation   she had been so afraid of rejection by this child   but it had boomeranged and now she was sure he would die and it was all her fault   "don't be silly" said whitney   "you can go and see him at the hospital"   she shook her head

We are in the transit lounge for three quarters of an hour. They call the flight number. I follow the other passengers to the departure gate, where I surrender the boarding pass that is stiff from being clutched between my fingers. We board the plane in an orderly manner, filing behind one another to be vouched for by a flight stewardess' smile.

*David was in the hospital for many anxious months   she
visited him regularly   at first he suffered her visits with
inscrutable politeness   he grew thinner and weaker   his skin
was so pale it was translucent   she brought him story books,
coloured pencils, toy trains, mechanical toys, a jack-in-the-box
that brought the colour momentarily to his cheeks   he did
not smile   "you first" he seemed to say   "you first"*

We are airborne again. I watch the plane climbing and I know
I must reconcile myself to all that was, and is, and that is to be. For
my sake. For Whitney's sake. The doctor, who is a kind, gruff,
greying man, says that there is some justifiable guilt one must live
with in our lives. They are either the sins of omission or commis-
sion.

But there are some things my mother will never know. I don't
even know if she will understand. Either why it happened or why I
still brood, sometimes, late at night. When Whitney is not there to
reassure me, wake me from my nightmares.

My mother is curious. Naturally enough. I have written only
that his name is Whitney. But she is happy. She thinks all girls
should marry. And sooner rather than later.

But I shall never tell her about a little boy of eleven with his
large limpid eyes and the mongrel he loved. I will speak about
teaching in an English school, about English children, the Negroes
and the Irish. I will tell her what it is like. But I have already
mentioned this in my letters home.

She will never read between the lines.

25

Wedding Night

Gopal Baratham

His long stay in Britain had made him unaccustomed to the heat which he resented as much as driving two hundred miles to attend the wedding of a cousin he barely knew. But when his father, who was dying of cancer, said, "Krishna, I am too ill to travel. You, my eldest son, will have to represent us at your cousin Gopal's wedding," the will to offer excuses deserted him. He feared arriving more than the drive. His absence of several years would provoke even his most distant relatives into a kind of frenzy that only Tamils were capable of. And they were at their very best at weddings. Funerals, at least, were predictable: unconcealed self-pity climaxed by incineration and hysterics. But at weddings he could be certain of only one thing. The exact nature of the emotional outburst would be as unpredictable as it was inevitable.

In his seven years abroad Krishna had cultivated a belief in the sanctity of privacy and developed an abhorrence of demonstrativeness, an attitude which had significantly contributed toward his acceptability in Britain. He pursued under all circumstances a policy of non-intervention in the affairs of others and, if commitment was demanded, assumed an indifference which he felt was the only basis for a civilised society. At the wedding, however, he was sure to be bombarded with intimate inquiries about his personal life. Moreover, several older members of the family would impose upon him their views on how he should improve it. He would, he supposed, get by with noncommittal smiles and would, if they got too near the bone, exercise the restraint he had learnt in Britain. What he dreaded most was the outrageous behaviour to which Tamils felt committed at weddings. Tears, intimate exposés, hysterics, drunkenness, unwarrant-

27

ed affection or animosity—every known form of histrionic display and several new ones which the more creative members of the family would improvise for the occasion.

He had been driving his father's car for over four hours. Very early on he realised that the ancient vehicle had an individuality of its own. Its speed bore no relationship whatsoever to the pressure he applied to the accelerator but varied according to some whim of its internal combustion processes which were punctuated by intermittent detonations. Each of these filled the car with fumes which mingled with the damp warm air so that his breathing began to resemble that of a drowning man. A sudden silence and the knowledge that his breathing had returned to normal made Krishna aware that the car had stopped. Fiddling with the largely anonymous knobs on the dashboard, he had earlier discovered, was not only useless but could prove decidedly unpleasant. At the outset of his journey he had, when the car appeared to stall, pulled at a knob which faded capital letters designated the "choke." The interior of the car was promptly filled with sulphurous smoke and Krishna concluded that the manufacturers had included that particular knob in an era when the pun and practical joke were fashionable.

He got out and tried to hail passing cars. His attempts turned out to be near-disasters, for each of their drivers seemed unswerving in their determination to run him down. Quite suddenly the sun dropped behind the trees that lined the road, then disappeared altogether. The surrounding jungle, monotonous by daylight, became sinister and threateningly filled with the sounds of invisible animals. He was alone and afraid. The country and people he had tried to disown were taking revenge. Filled with fear and its inseparable accomplice, humiliation, he decided to abandon the wedding altogether. He would lock himself up in the car for the night, head for Singapore in the morning, and get back to Britain at the earliest possible opportunity.

Ten minutes after he had made this decision a van stopped behind him. Its driver, a fat Chinese, laughed uproariously when Krishna explained his plight. Then miraculously he produced a length of rope with which he towed Krishna to a nearby garage.

The van driver regaled the garage mechanic with the story of Krishna's misfortunes. Both of them spent several minutes laughing before the mechanic who, with little more than a spanner and a screwdriver, brought the old engine to life. When Krishna attempted to pay them they waved aside his dollars, somehow implying that the amusement he had provided was payment enough for the small service they had rendered.

Krishna by now felt completely ostracised. He would never understand these people or this country. He must miss the wedding and return to Britain as soon as possible. He would call his uncle and make his apologies. The breakdown was a blessing. The mechanic directed him to a telephone and after a lengthy discussion with an operator, whom the generous would describe as mentally retarded, he was connected to his uncle's home. He explained his plight to a voice at the other end which said, "Wait." There was the murmur of discussion in the background before the voice returned. "If you're not sure your car can make it, we'll send a car to get you."

"But you don't understand. I must be at least fifty miles away."

"Wait." A further murmur of discussion before the voice returned, saying, "We'll wait for you to come before we begin the wedding dinner."

"But I may be hours getting there. I may never arrive . . ."

"That's alright," said the voice, and hung up.

With a resignation born of fatigue he started the car. To his surprise the engine seemed to function better than it did before the breakdown and within an hour he was at his uncle's home.

Krishna had often heard the Tamils described as a vociferous and colourful people. The description does them a grave injustice. The Tamils can, using the simple elements of light, colour, and the human voice, create a kaleidoscopic babel of unimaginable proportions. The scene that greeted him as he entered the house fulfilled his worst expectations. A marquée had been set up in the garden that adjoined the living room. The canvas of the marquée was barely visible under the bunting, paper streamers, and balloons which decorated it. Coloured bulbs hung around the edge. Many of these flashed on and off to produce the effect of a Christmas tree, though Krishna was sure that the effect was not deliberate but merely the result of faulty wiring. Hidden under all this were loudspeakers which produced loud and electronically distorted Tamil music. The guests, sitting at the tables which filled the marquée, conversed in shouts as each attempted to be heard above the voices of his neighbours and the music of the loudspeakers. The volume of the loudspeakers was increased so that the music could be heard above the din. The guests spoke louder so they could hear each other over the music. Even as he stood watching them Krishna noted an escalation in the noise level. Judging by their demeanour several guests had attempted to still the pangs of hunger by consuming alcohol. A garland was placed round his neck. This gesture drew a cheer from the crowd. His uncle and aunt introduced him to several guests and a variety of cousins with vaguely familiar faces. There was much drinking ("rejoicing at his arrival" his uncle called it) before he was led to his table and dinner.

Asian guests, Krishna remembered, are obliged to display an uninhibited appreciation of the food and drink provided. The people around him fulfilled their obligations with gusto. They coughed and hiccupped, belched and farted, sometimes singly and sometimes in chorus, providing audible and odiferous evidence of their enjoyment. The food was washed down with large amounts of alcohol, and Krishna very quickly acquired a hazy nonchalance about his surroundings. He was vaguely aware that his cousin Venket, acting as a sort of master-of-ceremonies, announced that someone would make a speech. The conversation became somewhat muted and the tape recorder which provided the background music was turned off.

The speaker was a squat and rather deformed-looking man called Subramaniam. He had full cheeks, protruding eyes, and a magnificent moustache whose ends drooped toward the lapels of the loud checked jacket that he wore. His nose had begun by being uprightly aquiline but following the example of his moustache fell toward his full lips which were a disconcerting scarlet. For a moment, Krishna feared that Tamil men, notorious for their use of women's perfumes, had taken to using lipstick. Then he realised that the colour of Subramaniam's lips was produced by the mixture of betel leaf and lime which he chewed. Venket had introduced Subramaniam as being "revered and erudite." The reason for reverence and the nature of his erudition were not revealed. From the speech that followed, Krishna appreciated that these omissions, if deliberate, were wise.

Subramaniam spoke at a constant shout, neck veins distended. His diaphragmatic control was of the kind which opera singers reserved for the culmination of arias. He began by addressing the "revered," "exalted," and "honourable" elders present by their full names which often ran into twelve syllables. He then listed, again by name, all those who were absent. Krishna knew that several of the absentees were long since dead but this in no way prevented Subramaniam from providing lengthy and disarmingly cogent excuses for their absence. Preamble complete, he began. "Friends . . ." His hands groped for a word but found his glass instead and from this he took a generous gulp. "Friends," he repeated, "and neighbours. We live [he pronounced it 'lew'] in a dangerous age when time-honoured practices and customs enshrined by religion are threatened. Marriage is a joke and divorce [he pronounced it 'die worse'] an institution. But the parents of the groom are honourable people. They will not see this holy union defiled by Western inventions like French . . ." Pause. His groping hands found his miraculously refilled glass which he downed before continuing, ". . . like French devices. After all, the purpose of marriage is to produce children. Already good news is on the way."

Krishna found this revelation unnecessary and offensive but the gathering did not share his views. The men greeted this announcement with applause while the maidens exchanged surreptitious smiles and the matrons knowing looks.

Subramaniam continued, "This is a love [pronounced 'lough'] marriage and only a token dowry was paid. We Indians know about love. Love will lift the girl up and cast her down. Yes, love will cast her down like . . . like a ton of bricks. Love will penetrate her. Love will ascend and descend in her. Yes, my friends, ascend and descend, descend and ascend, ascend and descend." Trapped in his imagery Subramaniam repeated the words several times, swaying backward and forward as he did in a kind of coital rhythm which embellished, albeit unnecessarily, the intention of his words. "Yes," he screamed, "and from her loins shall flow . . ."—he paused and gulped his drink before continuing—"like the waters of the Ganges . . ." He paused again for a gulp. ("What?" Krishna wondered in horrified expectancy. He was beginning to believe that Subramaniam's pauses were deliberately designed to increase his own anxiety.) "Like the waters of the Ganges," he shouted. Then, realising that he had not divulged what would flow from the bride's loins, dropped his voice to a whisper and added, "Children. A river of grandchildren for my revered friends, the groom's parents. From between these thighs will gush the flood of the future."

Thunderous applause greeted the last statement. Krishna struggled to see what effect the speech with its revelation of her premature pregnancy had on the bride but the canopy which draped the bridal couch hid her face from him completely. His attention was then drawn to the activities which were occurring around the speaker. Subramaniam had not, as far as he was concerned, finished and Venket and a group of men were trying to persuade him otherwise. Some were pulling him down while others literally attempted to drown his hoarse protests with whisky. Suddenly his protests stopped. It was impossible to say if this was the result of asphyxia or intoxication. At the same time people began to disperse. The more Westernised shook hands while the traditional placed palm to palm in farewell *namaskharams*.

Krishna wandered into the living room which was now occupied entirely by members of the family. His uncle lolled on a cane setter. His face was bloated and red, suggesting that drink only enhanced the puffiness of some underlying glandular disorder. His dhoti, loosely wrapped around his waist, was in danger of being displaced by his distended belly.

"Krishna," he called, "come and sit beside your old and dying uncle and drink with him." He gestured to his youngest son Sridar who produced two full glasses of whisky. Krishna, feeling the effects of the alcohol he had already consumed, compliantly collapsed into a space beside his uncle, who promptly took a large swallow from his own glass and forced Krishna to do likewise.

"What does it feel like to be home after ten years? I hear you took all that time to fail your medical examinations?"

"I did not actually fail, uncle. I just changed my course to microbiology which I am still . . ."

"Alright, alright," the old man guffawed, "no need to be ashamed of failure when you're with your own flesh and blood. Ten years gone," he mused, shaking his head sadly.

"Only seven, uncle . . ."

"No need to be clever with me, young man. I was around when you were still swimming in your father's balls. Anyway, what does a failed doctor feel about this pregnant woman becoming his cousin?" He turned as he spoke toward the bride who now sat on a low stool beside him.

"She's a married woman now, uncle."

"Ah yes. But she was pregnant before she was married."

32

"Does it really matter all that much now?"

"Do you know what she is called?" A cunning look crossed the bloated old face.

"No."

"Kumari. Kumari, the virgin. The pregnant virgin." The old man bellowed with laughter, his dhoti slipping further down as his mirth transmitted itself to his belly. "Just like the Christians," he said, consumed by mirth so profound that it was silent and betrayed only by the movements of his paunch.

His uncle finished his drink and indicated that Krishna do likewise. Krishna, whose responses were becoming automatic, did so, convincing himself that the old man was at least entitled to his last joke and drink. Sridar immediately refilled both glasses. He took a sip from his glass and was not surprised to find that it contained undiluted whisky. Turning, he was shocked to see that Kumari had prostrated herself before the old man and was pressing her forehead to his slippered foot. He gave his uncle an inquiring look.

"She has no relatives in this country. I am now her father, that is why . . ."

"That is why we should treat her kindly and like one of our own." Drink had emboldened Krishna sufficiently to interrupt his uncle.

"We do. It is our way that . . ."

"She has a good degree and is a worthy daughter. Worthy to bear the grandchildren of someone as revered as you."

Even as he spoke Krishna realised that he was slipping into the jargon of those strange people, some of whom he had, alas, to acknowledge as relatives. It must be the heat and the drink. Then much to his surprise and to his uncle's delight he took a large sip from his glass.

All this while Krishna was vaguely aware of his aunty who had been moving in and out of the group. She had not said anything and the purpose of her movements was not clear. He remembered her as one who, in the teeth of hopeless odds, persevered in the old ways. While he had no sympathy for her beliefs, he admired her tenacity and was rather drawn to the old girl because of this. Whatever else he might feel about her, she had a definite role in the family and community. At home she provided stability and continuity; at funerals she organised and comforted; at weddings she advised and rejoiced. As he watched her more closely he noticed something peculiar about her gait. The old lady was stumbling a bit and tended to waver. She must have had a stroke, he thought. Misery touched him. Soon she would be unable to perform the functions for which she felt herself to be designated. What on earth would she do then? He thought of offering her his arm but his body seemed unable to make the effort the gesture demanded. Instead, he finished his drink, the bulk of which appeared to have evaporated in the heat.

"She is not of our caste."

Krishna looked up to find his aunty teetering before him in a manner which left no doubt as to the cause of her infirmity. "Caste, aunty?" he said. The word, long unheard, momentarily puzzled him. Then realising its implications he said, "But she has become one of us by marriage." Seeing that his words had little effect on his aunt he continued, "You have a beautiful new daughter. A girl who has a degree and will soon give you a grandson."

"I'm sure she got her degree the same way that we will get our grandson," his uncle intervened.

At this point somebody hit his uncle. It must have been the groom, Gopal, but he could not be sure of it, for no sooner had the implications of the remark dawned on him than pandemonium broke out around the old man. With a hoarse cry and as much agility as her condition allowed his aunty leapt toward the group, comprising mainly her sons, who appeared to have fallen on uncle.

"I'll show you where you came from!" she cried, spread-eagling her legs and lifting up the folds of her sari. Two of her daughters rushed forward to restrain her. "And he," she screamed, "put you there." She collapsed into the arms of her girls, sobbing. "And for what you have all done to my body this is the reward I get."

Krishna edged to the far corner of the settee. He was not, whatever happened, prepared to get involved in this drunken family brawl. Slaps and shouts were exchanged. Several of his sons were attempting to simultaneously embrace the old man, and the fracas appeared to be now largely over a question of priorities. Venket, who was the most sober, appealed to Krishna to intervene but this he smilingly declined to do.

He was wondering how he could extricate himself from the scene unnoticed when his attention was drawn to the bride, Kumari. She too appeared to have similar plans for she had half risen and was looking around her. Krishna tried to catch her eye. He hoped that his own discomfiture would in some small way lessen her isolation. But Kumari's furtive eyes sought nothing but escape. After confirming that the family were totally involved with each other she quietly back-pedalled into the darkness of the garden.

The family still heaved and hung together but affection had now replaced hostility. The sound of kisses replaced those of slaps, endearments instead of insults. Finally they disentangled themselves and glasses were replenished. "Come join us, Krishna," said his uncle. "Notwithstanding your stay in England and your failure, you are one of us."

Sridar, the youngest son, produced two full glasses of whisky and clinked his own against Krishna's. "Drink with us, brother," he said, swallowing half his glass. Fearing refusal would provoke animosity, Krishna obliged. He immediately regretted this for he appeared to lose control not only of his legs but of his whole body, and sprawled across the settee, his head nestling sweatily against his uncle's paunch. Gopal, who occupied an identical position on the other side of the old man, suddenly shouted, "More drinks, Kumari. Your husband and your father command you."

"But where is Kumari?"

"Kumari!"

"Kumari!"

Everyone rose to look for the bride.

"My bride, my new bride," Gopal wailed. "What about our wedding night?"

"I thought that was long over and done with," said uncle flatly.

Gopal threw a punch at his father's head. He was so drunk that he missed completely and his elbow curled round his father's neck. What had begun as an assault culminated in an embrace and clasping each other they fell on the couch.

This fresh explosion caused Krishna to sober up slightly. His legs felt steadier and after standing for a while to test them he began, like Kumari, to back out of the room. His first thought when out of it was to look for Kumari. He was outraged on her behalf and felt he must communicate this to her. She must know that there was at least one normal person in the family into which she was being married. Above all she must not feel alone. He searched the garden. It was dark and filled with sinister jungle sounds. Mercifully it was small

35

and, not finding the bride in it, he was able quickly to return to the house. He explored all the bedrooms including the bridal chamber which contained a large four-poster. No Kumari. The toilet was empty except for a half-full glass of whisky which he drank. Suddenly the urge for sleep became uncontrollable. He had driven over two hundred miles. He was unaccustomed to the heat. It had been a long and exhausting day. Under the staircase was a space in which there was a sheet and a half-full sack of rice. This he placed on its side and patted into the shape of a pillow. He then spread out the sheet and lay on it. He felt he should take off his shoes but he was very sleepy. In his present environment that kind of delicacy was unnecessary.

He awoke to the sound of birds and human voices. The world swayed a little when he first stood up but soon righted itself. Apart from a slight ache in his elbows his body seemed undamaged. The festivities of the night appeared to be still in progress. He could hear his uncle's booming voice and the chorus of his cousins nearby. The best thing to do would be to sneak out before they discovered he had gone. A quick silent dash out of the house, a tedious drive to Singapore, then a blissful flight back to London.

As he came round the corner of the stairs he saw the family. They were seated round the breakfast table. Uncle sat at its head with Kumari beside him. The old man's hand idled affectionately on her shoulder. Without turning, uncle said, "So you're up at last, Krishna. Have breakfast before you leave. You didn't eat much last night." Gopal, who sat on the other side of his father, said, "Come on, you drunken head. You'll need some coffee at least."

He was reluctant to join them. In some intuitive way he felt that it was his presence which had triggered off the demonstration of the previous night. At the same time he was unwilling to concede, especially to himself, that the restraint he had espoused was unequal to the challenge of confronting them.

"And where," he asked provocatively, "did the bride sleep last night?"

Kumari beckoned him to her; then pulling his ear down to the level of her mouth, whispered, "Under the bridal bed . . ." Then, his ear still beside her mouth, shouted, "With my husband, of course."

"And where else should a bride sleep?" Gopal asked his family.

"Making the clever and beautiful child that will be an old man's pride," uncle said, gesticulating for more coffee.

Kumari filled uncle's and aunty's cups.

"A lovely girl," said aunty.

"When duty is obvious, compliments are unnecessary, mother," said Kumari.

As Krishna nursed his coffee, he felt very much on his own. He could see that the family was secure. Groom was now husband; bride, wife and daughter. The demons of divisiveness had been formally exorcised.

Tanjong Rhu

Ho Minfong

The day after his mother was buried, Mr T. W. Li stood for a long time looking out of his office window high above Shenton Way. Below him, slivers of sunlight streaked the oily water of the Singapore harbour, as further away the muffled roar of rush-hour traffic droned on. Barely a quarter past five, and his office was utterly quiet: the throb of telexes stilled, the whirr of air-conditioners and neon lights turned off. It was time to go home.

And yet Mr Li was not ready to go. Despite the precision with which he invariably conducted his affairs, this afternoon Mr Li felt only a vague, uneasy desire to look out his office window a while longer. He was tired; his tie was, uncharacteristically, loosened and his collar unbuttoned. Still, like many of his contemporaries in a culture where ageing can still be a studied grace, Mr Li looked only as old as he chose to, his hair carefully dyed black except at the temples, where the streaks of grey gave him a distinguished look, as if he had inherited his wealth rather than made it.

That afternoon, however, Mr Li looked older than he would have wished. It was not that he was upset by his mother's funeral; that had been seen to quite properly. Her burial clothes were of gold brocade, her coffin carved from a single teak tree trunk, her funeral procession long, chaotic, and noisy. He had even remembered to have her jade bracelet and earrings put on before the lid was shut. She had looked just as she always did, imperturbable. Her yellowed skin was as delicately wrinkled as damp onionskin paper, stretched taut over her high cheekbones, and loosely over her mouth. Even in the casket, she was smiling the puckered smile of the toothless.

Mr Li sighed, and looked out the window. A jagged semicircle of ships was anchored below him, each awaiting its turn to be off-loaded at the wharves. There had been 68 of them yesterday, Mr Li remembered, and 84 the day before. Then he realised that, although he must have counted them as usual that morning, he could not remember the number for today.

Disconcerted, he reached for the pair of binoculars on the windowsill, and trained them onto the far left of the bay, where the huge DBS Building towered above the other skyscrapers. Three freighters, a cluster of tankers, huge container ships—one by one he counted them until he had methodically covered the entire sweep of the harbour, 78—that was the number for today. He repeated it to himself with satisfaction. Numbers were strong, numbers he could hold onto. Seventy-eight ships, 18th floor, 63 years old, like the co-ordinates of some private graph, these numbers anchored him in space and time.

He weighed the binoculars in his hand. He had bought them for his mother—one of the many things that, in the course of his increasingly successful business career, he had offered to her, and which she had left untouched until he gradually claimed them for his own. The binoculars had been for her cataracts, he remembered, a feeble attempt to persuade both himself and her doctor that an operation could be forestalled.

He had been boyishly impatient to show her these binoculars the evening he returned home from work with them. Barely waiting until his driver had stopped the Benz, and brushing aside the servant who had laid out his slippers for him, Mr Li had marched toward the back of his house in search of his mother. Through the living room, dining room, and study, his shoes had made sharp staccato sounds on the marble floors. Proud as he was of the house, Mr Li could never quite get over the feeling that there were too many empty rooms, and most of them too big.

In the pantry he had encountered Helen, sipping tea with a handful of her friends. He shied away from these teas of hers, with their soft chatter, the smell of perfume, the tarts made with imported strawberries.

"Edward," she had said, crossing her legs, "come and join us?"

He had mumbled a refusal, but as he backed away the pair of binoculars bumped loudly against his briefcase. Helen looked up with interest, and asked what they were.

"Oh, these," he said. "I picked them up today. For the children." He avoided her arched eyebrows and added lamely, "They never outgrow these things." *names anglicized*

"Really, Edward," his wife had said, amused. She turned to her friends and smiled. "Here our son's almost through Cambridge, and Ying about to leave for New York next month, and still he buys toys for them!" There was an obliging ripple of feminine laughter as he left the room.

He had found his mother beside the swimming pool in the back yard. Dappled by shadows of the papaya tree, she was feeding her chickens. A thin figure, slightly stooped, she was tossing a shower of millet around her. Wisps of grey hair, worked free from the bun at the nape of her neck, softened her high forehead and bony cheeks.

"Ah-Ma," he called.

She lifted her eyes and stared blankly at him. Cloudy with the pale thickness of accumulated years, her eyes stared at everything the same way, calm and blank like skyscraper windows.

"Ah-Ma, I bought—today—one thing, for you." As always when he switched from a day's usage of English back to Cantonese, he felt tongue-tied, even shy. *only a day*

She smiled at him. "Ah-Wah," she said, "things you can buy, I do not need." Her voice was low, almost guttural, but with the tonal lilt particular to Cantonese when it is spoken gently.

"But you don't even know what it is."

"I know I have everything I need."

"Everything, Mother? What about eyesight? Wouldn't you like to see?"

"Who says I can't see now?" she said sharply. "Is it that young doctor? Just because I wouldn't tell him what shapes were on that silly wall-poster of his?"

"You want to see *better*, don't you?" he amended quickly.

"I am not, Ah-Wah, having my eyes sliced open," she said.

"I'm not talking about the operation, Ah-Ma . . ."

"Like a clove of garlic or what, talking about peeling my eyes!" *word order*

"This has nothing to do with the operation," he said, and thrust the binoculars into her free hand. "They're special glasses, big ones to help you see things faraway."

"See-far glasses? What do I want to look at faraway things for?" She tossed a handful of millet to the chickens, clucking softly to them.

He looked at her, this papaya-shaped old woman whose womb, like the seed cavity of the fruit, had held countless seeds within it. Mother of nine, grandmother of thirty-four, great-grandmother of seventeen, her seeds had burst out from her and planted themselves in ripples of concentric circles around her. And she, rivetted at their centre, held them together. Now, in the back yard of her eldest son's house, she spent her evenings scattering grain to a brood of chickens. What, after all, would she need these binoculars for? He kicked aside a hen which was scuffing at his shoe, and turned back toward the house.

Without even looking up, she had sensed his retreat. "Wait," she called after him. "Those see-far glasses of yours, can they see Tanjong Rhu?"

He stopped. "Tanjong Rhu?" he hesitated, frowning. "I suppose so—depends where you're looking from, of course."

"If they can see as far away as Tanjong Rhu," she said, "I will try them."

He walked back to her, the eagerness growing in him again. "From my office window, Ah-Ma," he said quickly, "if you stand right at the end of the room, you can see Tanjong Rhu very clearly." He tugged at her wide sleeve to stop her from tossing her handfuls of grain. "I'll take you up there—you've never even been to my office—and we'll look through the see-far glasses at Tanjong Rhu. Would you like that?"

"I would," she said. "I have not seen your father's shipyard for a long time."

"Father's shipyard?"

"The one at Tanjong Rhu. Don't you remember?"

"But Mother, that was torn down years ago. Thirty years ago!"

She shook her sleeve free of him. "You said those see-far glasses could see faraway, Ah-Wah," she chided.

"Oh, Mother," he sighed.

It was beginning to get dark. Her arm hung limp by her side, a trickle of grain slipping through her fist. A passing breeze fluttered against the wide sleeves and loose trousers she wore. "Not that I really need those glasses anyway," she said. "I can see Tanjong Rhu well enough." She paused for emphasis. "Behind my eyes."

"Yes, Ah-Ma," he said, backing away.

"You remember?" she asked. "You used to climb inside the

42

empty hulls of the fishing boats your father was building, playing hide-and-seek with Ah-May and Ah-Lian?"

"The mosquitos are biting, Mother. Let's go in."

"And that little shack we lived in, with the *attap* roof and wooden stilts poking into the mud, remember?" *doesn't seem nonstandard*

"I'm going in," he said.

She held onto his arm. "No, Ah-Wah, wait for me," she said *yet* softly. "I've finished now." She sprinkled what was left of the millet to the chickens, and turned her blank eyes up at him. "My cane, please," she said.

Instead he offered her his arm. Together, they walked across the sun-streaked lawn. She leaned heavily on him, but her steps were small and sure. At the entrance of the house she paused while a servant opened the door for them. "Maybe I *will* go take a look," she said, as if making a major concession. "Even if I cannot see where your father worked, I could see where you work."

The servant tried to usher her through the door into the air-conditioned coolness within, but she resisted, tightening her hold on his arm. "Tomorrow morning, then," she promised. "I will go with you to your office, to take a look. Maybe we'll see Tanjong Rhu after all?" She threw him a backward glance over one thin shoulder, and stepped inside.

The next morning, on his way downstairs for breakfast, he caught a glimpse of her in the dim little room where the family altar was tucked away. "Ah-Ma," he called down to her, "are you really coming with me today?"

There was no reply. He paused to watch her putter around the altar. Doing everything by touch, she had dusted the altar shelf, replaced the wilted flowers on it with fresh hibiscus from the garden, and was now sweeping the tiled floor. He tried to talk to her again, but this time she cut him short.

"If something is to be done," she said with the loud solemnity which she reserved for the altar room, "it must be done properly. If I am to visit your place of work, I must tell your father of it properly." Carefully, she unlocked the top drawer of her mother-of-pearl inlaid cabinet, where she kept all the paraphernalia for tending the altar: tiny porcelain winecups, gold-leafed sheets of ceremonial money, candles and joss sticks and countless packets of incense. There had been a time when her grandchildren, their noses barely

43

reaching above the drawer, had been fascinated by its contents. On festival days they would cling to her, asking to help fill the winecups, or to fold the gold sheets into the horned bars of traditional Chinese money. Ying especially had loved to follow her grandmother's example, gleefully setting the gold money on fire before the altar, then smothering its ashes with cups of wine.

"Baba," he heard Ying call now, "your noodles are getting cold!"

Obediently, he left the doorway to the altar room and headed for breakfast. Only after he had finished his second cup of coffee and read through the *Asian Wall Street Journal* did he send Ying to hurry her grandmother up. "Tell her I'm leaving in five minutes," he said. "See to it she's ready by then."

Minutes later, he glanced impatiently at his watch. It was 8:34 and there was still no sign of either his mother or his daughter. He tossed his newspaper aside and went back to the altar room. He found the two of them tussling over a bouquet of joss sticks.

"Let me do it, Popo," Ying was saying. "You do it so slowly."

"And you don't know how to do it at all," her grandmother retorted, holding onto the joss sticks.

"There's nothing to it. It's simple."

"Yes? How many times do you bow after lighting the incense?"

"What does it matter? Come on, Popo, I've seen you do it often enough. Let me do it and get it over with." She noticed her father in the doorway, and winked at him. Softly, in English, she said to him, "This is going to take forever!" Then, reverting back to Cantonese, she tried cajoling her grandmother to hurry up by letting her do it. "Grandfather would probably enjoy hearing from me for a change," she said. "You're the only one to talk to him."

"And do you even know how to address your grandfather? Do you think he can hear you if you prattle to him in that silly way of yours? And how do you say what you want to say? Afterward what candles do you light, what wine do you offer, what incense do you burn?" She tilted her chin defiantly at the young girl, tendrils of smoke from the joss sticks spiralling from her hands. "What? Does the little monkey fall silent when the tiger roars?"

Ying sighed elaborately. "My father's waiting for you. He'll be late for work."

"Tell him," the old lady replied stiffly, "that *his* father is waiting for me!"

Retreating to the doorway, Ying whispered conspiratorially, in English, to her father, "She's so darn stubborn, Baba. Always has to have her own way!"

Impatient as he might have been with the rituals his mother was performing, he found himself resenting Ying's remark still more. He especially resented the fact that it had been in English. "She's old," he announced in Cantonese, "she has eaten more salt than you have rice."

He looked at the faded photograph of his own father, propped up on the altar shelf, flanked by a pair of electric candles which glowed with pink lightbulbs. For years his mother had refused to use anything but real candles, and it was only after she had almost set fire to the whole altar that she finally agreed to change to these electric things.

The joss sticks clasped between her palms, the old woman bowed stiffly before the altar. "Hear me, respected father of my son," she called, in a voice which seemed both intimate and formal, "Ah-Wah is taking me to see his place of work today, a beautiful room with windows at the edge of the sky."

Ying shook her head, and tried to slip away. Her father grabbed her by the arm and stopped her. "You stay and listen to this," he whispered.

"He is getting richer and richer," she said, "and his office rises higher and higher off the ground, on top of the sea." She lifted thin arms to jab the joss sticks into the bronze urn full of ashes, her bracelets making a sweet clinking sound on her wrists. "He says he can see Tanjong Rhu from there, so I will go up and look for it too. Perhaps, father of Ah-Wah, I will see you there."

The photograph of the man—ten years younger when he died than his son was now—looked down at him. The image was yellowed now, and what wrinkles might have been on the face were now blurred, so that he looked strangely ageless. Suddenly Li felt an impulse to talk to his own father again, to rattle off in clipped Cantonese rambling accounts of his thoughts, his feelings. But his tongue seemed stuck, unable to curl around syllables which by now seemed almost unfamiliar. Mutely, then, he watched his mother shuffle back to the cabinet to put away the matches and incense, and mutely he watched her lock the drawer.

She had not been able to see any of the freighters, of course, even with the binoculars. Standing at his office window, she had held onto them so tightly that the veins pulsed green between her knuckles, as she had squinted into them.

"It's lovely," she had said, without conviction. A few clouds grazed in the blue sky, but there was nothing else. A faint smell of incense lingered on her hair.

"Not there, Ah-Ma," he said. "Look down."

Dutifully she lowered her head and directed the binoculars downward. Her opaque gaze followed vaguely. "Oh yes, I think I see . . . well, what am I supposed to see, anyway?"

"The freighters, Mother. Can't you see the big cargo ships out in the harbour?"

"Cargo ships?"

"There, Ah-Ma. They're right in front of you." How could she not see them, he thought, when I count them every morning even without the stupid glasses?

"Many of them, Ah-Wah," she said, "everywhere they are." But she had moved her head away from the binoculars and was staring blankly, straight in front of her.

Almost roughly, he pressed her head back down toward the binoculars, making her hold onto them more steadily. The veins seemed thicker and greener on her fists, pulsing desperately.

"Look through them," he commanded. "Can't you see faraway? The whole view of the harbour?"

Dubiously she nodded, her eyes peering around the rims of the lenses at him again.

"Not me, Mother! Out there! What do you see?"

She hesitated. "Nothing," she finally said.

Desperately he swivelled her around, directing her face to the far right of the bay, where the four-lane Pan-Island Expressway cut through the mushrooming Housing Development Board highrises. "That's Tanjong Rhu over there, Mother. Can you see it? Those glasses are powerful, Ah-Ma. You must be able to see *something*?"

There was a long pause as she remained unblinking behind the binoculars. Then she smiled, pressing her eyes tight against the lenses. "Oh yes," she beamed. "I see, I see it now."

"What, Ah-Ma?"

"A skinny little boy," she said, her voice trembling, "in a dirty shirt and torn khaki shorts. Barefoot, too, on the beach, walking by

himself. Skipping pebbles on the waves, mumbling to himself, counting the fishing boats anchored near the Tanjong Rhu shipyard." She
laughed, and her laugh was vibrant and subtly teasing. "I see you,
Ah-Wah, I see you so clearly."

"Mother," he said, and tried to pull the binoculars away from
her. Her grip only tightened.

"I see our *attap* hut by the sea, among the half-built hulls of
fishing boats. And the walkway of planks leading out to the out-
house over the sea. You liked that so much, didn't you? Used to
squat over that hole in the board for hours at high tide, craning your
little neck to watch the catfish swim in to nibble at your shit . . ."

"Stop it, Ah-Ma," he said, brusque now.

"And I see myself too. My pants are rolled up to the knees—
your father would have been so shocked!—and I'm walking on the
shoreline where the seaweed has been swept up by the sea. There's
that old rattan basket on my arm, half-filled with soft-shelled crabs
that you and I have caught, scuttling among the seaweed. How you
run! On all fours like a crab yourself, digging quick into the wet sand
after the crabs!"

"That's enough, Mother," he said. "Give those glasses back to
me now."

Without resistance this time, she handed the binoculars back to
him. And when she raised her eyes to his, they were as blank as the
office windows reflecting the morning sunlight, and the smile had
faded from her dark, wrinkled face.

He looked at the binoculars on the windowsill now. There was
a thin film of dust on the lenses, and gently he wiped it away. In the
hall outside his office, a phone was ringing softly, but he hardly
noticed it. Ah-Ma, he thought, what could you see that morning?
Was it really our Tanjong Rhu?

Suddenly he was seized with a longing so sharp his eyes stung.
He wanted to see a fleet of fishing boats at dusk, streaming into the
piers at Tanjong Rhu, their tattered sails billowing in the wind, hulls
slapping against the waves. And in the cool mornings, they would
bob their silent way out again to sea, their full-bellied sides gleaming
with the interlaces of light reflected from the waves. Closer at home,
there would be the smell of salt and dried fish and rice porridge
cooking over charcoal fires.

And yes, he must have been barefoot then, because the sand

was damp and gritty between his toes, and the tendrils of seaweed which licked at his ankles, cold and slimy. word order

Had he always walked on that Tanjong Rhu shore by himself? Hadn't there been some hand, thick and calloused, that he held onto? A single big thumb, yes. And soft-shelled crabs, she said—did she cook those crabs? He remembered a big wok, shiny-smooth on the inside and encrusted with layers of soot on the outside, didn't the crabs get thrown into that? Sizzling with bits of scallions and dried chilli, until their shells turned as red as the chilli.

And she said I had counted fishing boats even then. How old was I? When was all this? Why has it all slipped away from me? I should have asked her then, he thought bitterly. I should have sat her down and talked to her. I should have listened.

When he had tried finally to ask her, she had already become inaccessible, faraway. Hospitalised for a cough which developed into pneumonia, and which in turn was complicated by jaundice, she lay propped on a pile of pillows, her face like some pomelo skin laid out on the pavement to dry. He saw the splint on her inner arm, strapping tubes of mauve-cool blood into her veins. Another tube, hooked up to a metallic tank, fed oxygen into her nostrils; yet a third was connected vaguely beneath the grey blanket, and dripped tea-coloured urine into a plastic bag.

His daughter Ying was there, combing the tangled wisps of grey hair back from her grandmother's ears. She straightened up as her father entered, and clasped onto the iron railing around the bed. She looks so proprietary, he thought, as if she was some mother with a newborn. And indeed, the hospital bed looked like an oversized crib: grandmother as a baby.

Ying smiled at him. "Popo's better today," she said. "She drank some chicken broth and I donated a pint of blood."

He ignored the comment, put down the basket of large purple orchids he had bought in the hospital lobby, walked back to close the door, then decided to leave it ajar. He hated hospital rooms; he always felt trapped by them.

"She had dozens of visitors today, and she could recognise some of them," Ying said, bending back to comb the grey hair. "Second aunt came in with some shiny brocade stuff she said would be Popo's burial clothes. She wanted to put it under Popo's pillow, but I wouldn't let her. We had quite a fight. They're in the closet now.

Second Aunt refused to take them back with her." Ying stopped and looked up at him, and her eyes were uncertain. "She's not going to die, is she?"

He walked up to the bed. A faint smell of sweat and cologne reached him. "Can't you open the damn window?" he asked irritably.

Ying flung down the hairbrush and went to push open the one window in the room. A hum of traffic noises and a rush of warm twilight air blew in. Turning, she said to him, "You haven't said hello to her yet. Maybe she'll recognise you. You should try it, Baba."

She steered him until he was directly in front of the old up-turned face. "She's asleep," he said, feeling relieved.

"No, she isn't," Ying said. "She keeps her eyes closed all the time, that's all. I think she's too tired to open them. But she can see, if I hold them open. Watch." She slipped behind her grandmother, and carefully pulled the loose-flesh eyelids up, with two careful forefingers. The old woman's eyes gazed out at him, their dull sheen like scratched opal. Unblinking, she stared.

"Go on, Baba. Say something, hurry!"

"Ah-Ma," he began, feeling stupid. "I'm here. Can you hear me?"

Her eyes, held apart by Ying's fingers, were intense yet faraway. As if she were looking through those binoculars, he thought. Then, from deep within that cavity which had once nurtured him, a single sound welled up. "Ah-Wah," she said, her voice rich and hollow.

"See? See? She recognised you," Ying said excitedly. "Now ask her something. Talk to her."

Ask her something. He cleared his throat. "Ah-Ma," he hesitated, wishing Ying would leave the room. "Ah-Ma, when I was little . . ."

"Louder," Ying whispered.

"When we lived at Tanjong Rhu, Ah-Ma, did you take me for walks? Did you really count fishing boats with me?"

Like bits of scratched opal, those eyes.

And was it you who carved toy boats out of bits of driftwood, with sails of woodshavings? Did you cook the soft-shelled crabs we caught together? Was it you who began this game of counting ships, Mother, was it?

But he was as mute as she was blind.

49

He looked up at Ying, and scowled. "Let go of her eyelids," he snapped. "She's not a doll."

"But she likes . . ."

"Let go!"

One eyelid dropped down, a slow, elaborate wink. Then the other.

"Don't you have any respect for your elders? She's your grandmother, not some toy!" He was on safe ground now. "Playing with her eyes like that when she's dying . . ."

"She's *not* dying!" Ying protested loudly.

"You young people have no respect for . . ."

"I donated a pint of blood, didn't I? You old folks just give her burial clothes!"

"Ying, that's enough!"

Father and daughter confronted each other for a long moment. In the silence, a low moan from the head of the bed startled them both. Li turned to his mother, and noticed a tiny, fluttering movement near the pillows. Very feebly, her fingertips were tapping, as if groping for something. He reached over and held them still.

"Ah-Wah," she said, her lips barely moving, "the key . . ."

He looked at Ying questioningly.

"She's fretting about her keys again," Ying said impatiently, in English. "It's been on her mind all day. Probably something to do with those rusty old biscuit boxes she keeps her keys and loose change and junk in." Ying bent down to her grandmother's ear, and said loudly, in Cantonese, "Listen, Popo. I know where your boxes of keys are. I'll bring them here for you tomorrow, all right?"

The old head turned from one side of the pillow to the other, restlessly. "No," she managed to say. "The key to the altar, it's in a special place."

"She's just tiring herself like this," Ying said to her father. "Tell her to stop worrying. She'll listen to you."

"Ah-Ma," Li said, bending toward her. "Don't worry about it. It's all right. You rest now. Sleep." Still he felt her fingers fluttering underneath his. "Don't worry. The key is safe."

Her fingers gradually stopped moving, and became limp. He lifted his hand gently from hers. The green veins between her knuckles had stopped throbbing. Curled on the grey blanket, her hand had looked like a tiny cluster of sea anemone, left stranded on the sand by the low tide.

In the deepening twilight outside his office window, the sea was merging with the sky, with only a thin thread of silver at the horizon. Of course, he thought now, the altar. That last gesture of propriety to acknowledge her death: that was what he had forgotten to do. Mr Li put down the binoculars on the windowsill and straightened up. A few stray seagulls were swooping in arcs of pure grace over the harbour, but it was too dark to see the silent ships anchored further out at sea.

Mr Li turned away from the window. I have to go home, he thought. I have to do that one last thing for her, and then everything will be finished. With his sense of order regained, Mr Li straightened his tie and, briefcase in hand, left the office for home.

The altar room was cool and dark. The electric candles were unplugged, the joss sticks in the bronze urn long since burnt out. Without the smell of incense and fresh flowers, the room seemed empty, incomplete. Groping in the dim light, he found the switch to the plastic candles, and turned them on. A pale pink light suffused the room.

His father's face, bland and ageless as ever, stared out into the darkness. The red ancestral tablet, with three generations of Li's inscribed on it, was hung next to the photograph. Carefully, on tiptoe, he reached up and edged the photograph, the tablet, and the incense urn over to one side. In the space he had made, he propped up a framed photograph of his mother.

There, it was done. She was up there now, next to his father. Among the ancestors. He stepped back and looked at them both. "Ah-Ma," he began, then stopped. Awkwardly, stealing a glance at the empty doorway, he bowed once, a stiff ducking of his shoulders. Some joss sticks, he thought, I suppose I should light some joss sticks. He walked to the pearl-inlaid cabinet where she kept her paraphernalia of prayer. One by one, he yanked the drawers open, and rummaged through their contents: balls of string, mosquito coils, old slips of fortune-telling from temples long since torn down. There were no joss sticks.

In the uppermost right-hand corner of the cabinet, he tugged at a drawer that would not open. The joss sticks, he suddenly remembered, would be in there, where she kept her most precious things. He tugged at the handle again, but the drawer remained shut. And then he realised that she always kept it locked. And he did not know where she kept the key.

51

Through the window an evening breeze blew in, sweeping up a few stray flakes of ash from the incense urn into the air. As he watched, some ash landed against the photograph, on his mother's cheek.

He stretched up and carefully wiped the dark flake off. The glass surface was cool under his fingers. He remained standing on tiptoe for a moment longer, looking at the photograph.

"Ah-Ma," he whispered, and his voice resonated faintly in the room. "Ah-Ma, I saw Tanjong Rhu today." His voice broke. He stood there, arms limp at his sides, an elderly man in a grey business suit. What am I doing, he thought, talking in an empty room to an old photograph?

Abruptly he turned and walked out of the altar room. The electric candles glowed a pale pink on the altar, lighting up the faces of the two ancestors.

Monologue

Kirpal Singh

I am lying on an old mattress in the living room. All around
me is white. White walls. White built-in cupboards. White ceiling.
White window panes. White. I don't like white very much. Reminds
me too much of death. Or of purity. In my mind purity and death
have a similar reference point. Termination. My wife, however, likes
white. I wonder what she'll say when we move into another house
where my colour—my favourite is black—predominates. Right now
she is blissfully sleeping in the bedroom. Blissfully. She does not
know what's on my mind. No one does. I am my own master. I
keep my own secrets. But white irritates me. Gives me a headache.
Takes away my concentration. I get up and turn on the ceiling fan.
It is an old-fashioned fan. I like old-fashioned things. I lie again. It is
a hot afternoon and the sun is shining brightly outside. Even the day
is white. Because of this I have decided not to go to work this
afternoon. I am not sure whether it is the white alone which
prompted me not to go to work. I am lying down on an old mattress. It is a discarded one. But since the housing people don't want
to take it back I've let it lie here. For moments like these. It is quite
comfortable. Though I don't like to sleep on it, I like to lie on it. It
is a big mattress. And strong. And firm. As I lie on it my eyes gaze
into the ceiling. I see the fan going round round. Round and round.
Regularly. Monotonously. I see the fan. My mind does not see the
fan. My mind is thinking of something else. I try to concentrate on
the fan but I can't. My mind is too much for me. Outside the birds
are chirping away. There are all kinds of birds here. Cockatoos, gelas,
wagtails, crows, sparrows. Even an owl. But he is asleep I think. Like
me he too does not like white much. But the other birds are ob-

viously enjoying the sunshine. My house has a white fence around it. Not much of a fence—my neighbour's dog comes through it easily—but white nevertheless. Sometimes when I look up at the trees I see white birdnests on the white tree branches. Eucalyptus. Gum. White. I don't like white very much. As I lie down on my mattress I try to concentrate. But I can't. My mind gets too full of things. I hate Descartes. I think therefore I am not. My thoughts take me away from myself. They deny the real me. A fake me takes over. The real me just wants to stare endlessly into the fan as it goes round and round, round and round. The fake me is thinking of all kinds of things. I don't see the connection between the real me and the fake me. I stare into the ceiling fan. I see a little boy being followed by a woman in black. I do not know who she is. I don't think I know the boy either. But my mind is not seeing. My mind is thinking. It is now thinking of a line from Yeats. I think it comes from "The Second Coming." All about me reel shadows. Indignant. Because my mind does not see the little boy or the little woman. When I was young and living in Jalan Eunos our house had a small well at the back. The little boy is walking around this well. The woman in black is following. Nothing else seems to happen. Shadows appear. My mind is still thinking. It now has moved on to Tagore. It recalls the famous line from *Gitanjali*. Where the head is held high and the mind is without fear. I do not know what the line means. The real me is seeing the boy walking around the well. The woman in black is relentlessly following. The ceiling fan is going round and round, round and round. I go back to the time I was a boy. I see the well. I see it clearly. I look around. There is no one else beside me. And yet the woman in black is still following the little boy around the well. Am I seeing things? My mind is still trying to fathom the meaning of Tagore's line. Yeats and Tagore knew each other. Can the mind be without fear when there are indignant shadows about? Can the head be held high when the second coming is at hand? I think I'm beginning to feel drowsy. I don't seem to be making sense of the boy going round the well. But this mattress is not the one on which I like to sleep. My wife is sleeping in the bedroom. She does not know about this small boy. She did not see the well of my childhood. And my mind which should remember the well clearly is getting lost in strange and abstruse thoughts. The real me is still just lying down here, staring into the ceiling. Outside the birds are still chirping. I cannot be sure if the birds know what I know. Do they see the small boy around the well? I cannot be sure. But the woman is in black. Most of what is around me is white. I don't like white very much. When I was eight I went to school in a white pair of underpants. My teacher made fun of me. I went home crying. Maybe that was the end of white for me. Purity. Death. I can't be sure. Many things happened when I was small. I used to walk around the well at the back of my house in Jalan Eunos. My uncle used to ask me to get water for the dogs. We had Alsatian dogs and they drank a lot of water. But I used to walk round the well. The fan is going round and round. My mind is still thinking about Yeats and Tagore. I've never been at home with my mind. It thinks too much. Like now. I'm seeing the little boy and the woman in black. My mind is not. I hate Descartes. I think therefore I am not. I do not want to be predicated. I want to remain the subject. I want to lie down on this mattress and relax. After all I took off from work. I don't know why. But I am lying down on this old mattress. The birds have become quieter for some reason. Maybe they are getting fed up with the white around them. I don't like white very much. When I was eight I wore a pair of white pants to school. I remember the teacher—she was a pretty girl—held my pants and laughed. All the other boys laughed too. Since then I have not liked white underpants. My wife likes them. White. It comes between me and my wife. Now it is coming between me and the ceiling fan. As I see white, my mind is still engrossed on those two buffoons. I call them buffoons because they sang songs which made good melody but which nobody understood. We still await the second coming. We still cannot hold our heads up high. Our minds are still not without fear. I don't know what I am thinking or what I am seeing. It is getting rather confused. But I know I'm lying on an old mattress in my living room in my own house. My wife is blissfully sleeping in the next room. When my uncle used to ask me to get water for the dogs I used to be very happy. It gave me a chance to play near the well. I used to run round and round the well. I used to look inside the well. It was all very black inside the well. The woman in black is still going after the little boy round and round the well. I think I know who the little boy is. But I don't know who the woman is. But she is in black. And I love black. Black is the opposite of white. Opposite of purity. Opposite of death. I have never known my mother. I left her when I was a baby. She left me when I was a baby. We left each other. Alone. Alone, alone in a white white room. Coleridge is one of my favourite poets. I read him often. I remember he helped Mill come back to reality. I think Mill was a genius. I do not know if I am a genius. But I think the small boy going round and round the well is a genius. I think the woman in black following him is a genius too. Only geniuses do that sort of a thing. Going round and round, round and round. When I was a small boy my uncle used to ask me to get water from our well in our house in Jalan Eunos for our Alsatian dogs and I used to go round and round the well. I used to look inside the well. It was all very black inside the well. I think I am repeating myself. But my mind does not seem to be with me. It has finally got away from the literary figures of Yeats and Tagore. Outside my room I cannot hear the birds anymore. But my neighbour is playing on his piano. I like piano music. So I want to listen to him playing on the piano. I don't really know my neighbour. But I know his dog. Our fence is not very good because it allows our neighbour's dog inside our compound. My fan, old-fashioned as it is, is still going round and round. I remember when I was at the University I read a book in which it was said that if one stared at the ceiling for too long one could be hypnotised. Maybe I am being hypnotised by this old-fashioned fan. I love old-fashioned things. The little boy seems to have grown bigger somehow. And the lady older. I think I can now see her wrinkles. She seems to be carrying an umbrella. I wonder why. It is very hot. This is why I have turned on the fan. Outside the sun is shining brightly. My neighbor is still on his piano. I don't know what he is playing. Maybe Mozart. I love Mozart. I think Mozart was a genius. I think the little boy going round the well is a genius. My mind has strayed away from me. My mind is now thinking about writing a story. My real self is not a writer. My fake self is a writer. My mind is my fake self. I hate Descartes. I do not like to be predicated. My mind wants to predicate my senses. It wants to control my thoughts. But I want to keep staring at the fan as it goes round and round, round and round. Monotonously. I think life is like my old-fashioned fan. I think life is a genius like the little boy going round the well. I love life. I never knew who my mother was. When I was small my uncle used to ask me to get water from the well. I used to love playing near the well. One day I wore white underpants to school and my teacher laughed at me. The other boys laughed at me. My wife buys me white underpants. I hate wearing white underpants. I love black. The woman in black is carrying an umbrella. But it is hot. The sun is shining brightly outside. I think my neighbour has changed his tune. He has left Mozart and is now playing a piece by Chopin. I think Chopin was a genius. But I don't like Chopin. He reminds me of white. Purity. Death. I like black. This is why I cannot take my eyes off the woman in black. But my mind is pulling me away. My mind is making it difficult for me to concentrate on the fan. My mind is thinking about writing a story. My fake self is not a writer. I don't like white very much. My ceiling fan is old-fashioned and white. The ceiling is white. My wife is sleeping blissfully in the next room. She does not know what is in my mind. She does not know what is in store for her. I am my own master. I keep my own secrets. But I love black. I see a young man going round the well now. He is going round and round, round and round. The woman in black is still there. She is pointing her umbrella at the young man. She is very old now. She is not able to walk fast now. But she still holds her umbrella firmly. I don't know why she has an umbrella. It is hot outside. The birds have all gone away. My neighbour has stopped playing his piano. My fan is still going round and round. Weave a circle round it thrice. I love Coleridge. He brought Mill out of insanity. I think Coleridge was a genius. I think the old woman in black chasing the young man round the well is a genius. My mind is seriously making plans about writing a story. It is searching for a subject. I don't like my mind very much. When I was at the University my philosophy professor told me that the mind is a blank tablet. White. I don't like white very much. When I was only eight the boys in school laughed at me. My uncle used to tell me to get water for our dogs. My neighbour's dog comes into our compound through the fence. I am lying here in my living room on an old mattress. My long hair is getting sticky all over. I have long hair. I love long hair. Grinding at the mill, eyeless in gaze. I think Milton was a genius. I do not know if I am a genius. When I was small they did an IQ test on me. They never told me the results. Maybe I am a genius. I have long hair. I ask my wife to wash my hair every month. My hair is long and black. I love black. The old woman in black is still pointing her umbrella at the young man going round the well. My wife is sleeping in the next room. Somehow I never got to know my mother. When I was young I used to play near the well. Right now I think about the well in our house in Jalan Eunos. Both well and house are no more. But the little boy still goes round the well and the woman in black still struggles to catch him. I think I know who the boy is. He is a man now. I think my mind has got hold of an idea for a short story. My mind is forcing me to think. I think about the boy and the woman and the well. I think about my uncle and the teacher and the boys and white underpants. I think about Yeats, and Tagore and Coleridge and Milton. I think I am like Samson. Samson had long hair like me. I ask my wife to wash my long hair once a month. She does not like to do this. Now she is sleeping in the next room. She is sleeping on the mattress I like to sleep on. I am lying on this old discarded mattress here. The sun outside is still shining brightly. I don't like white very much. When I was young I wore white underpants. I love black. I think Mohammed Ali is a genius. Black is beautiful he said. I love black. The woman in black has stopped suddenly. The young man has disappeared. My mind is telling me to concentrate on the story it is thinking of writing. The fan is going round and round. Life is going round and round. I love life. I cannot see the connection between my mind and me. I hate Descartes. My real self wants to lie down and just look at the ceiling fan as it goes round and round. All around me is white. My mind is trying to hold my attention. It is telling me about a story it has thought about. I don't want to listen to my mind. I want to see what the old woman in black is going to do now that the young man is not there. I don't seem to be able to see the old woman clearly now. I think I am getting confused. I think I may be falling asleep. But I know I cannot sleep on this mattress. It is an old mattress and everything around me is white. I don't like white. White is purity. I am not pure. White is death. I don't think I am dead. But the old woman in black seems to be dying. She is beginning to change into white. I think the fan, being old-fashioned, is playing tricks on me. Everything about me is quiet. My mind is working at top speed now on the story it has thought for itself. My mind is telling me to get up and write it down before it loses the main thread of the story. But I took this afternoon off from work. I want to lie down and watch the fan going round and round. When I first lay down I saw a small boy going round and round the well with a woman in black following. Now the boy has disappeared. And the woman is changing into white. When I was young, in our house at Jalan Eunos, I used to play near the well at the back of the house. My wife seems to have woken up. I hear her calling my name. But I am not listening to her because I am feeling hot and I am busy watching the change in the woman in black. I have lost the small boy. Now I think I am going to lose the woman too. My long hair is really sticky. My wife wants to know if I want my hair washed. It is one month today. She does not know what is on my mind. The fan is going round and round. Monotonously. My mind is succeeding I think. It is telling me to get up and write a story. The story is about a small boy going round and round a well at the back of a house in Jalan Eunos. The small boy is being followed by a woman in black. All this is too much for me. I have to stop looking at the fan. My mind has taken over. I hate Descartes.

Another Country

Shirley Lim

When Su Weng regained consciousness, she was alone. Her head was helmeted in a swath of bandages, her right arm and hand disappeared into a roll of white cotton, and her left leg was raised by a pulley above the bed, the foot encased in a large wrap. Her bed was screened on two sides, and at the foot of the bed was only a blank white wall. A fat plaster sat on her right cheek partially blocking her vision.

"I say, you look like Pharaoh's mummy! I think you surely die when they bring you in. You look really terrible, lah!"

Su Weng painfully adjusted her aching neck toward the left from where the cheerful voice was coming. Dimly she was aware of a shapeless figure in a loose white gown half-hidden by the screen.

"What's your name, eh?" The white shape approached her bed.

"Mrs Hashim. Mrs Hashim! What are you doing here? You're not allowed in this room. The doctor is coming and he will be angry if he sees you here."

At the sound of this brisk voice coming from somewhere out of sight, the shape turned and vanished. Su Weng kept her neck strained waiting for someone else to appear, the nurse or doctor or some more familiar visitor. But no one came and soon she was drifting off into dark emptiness. At one point she woke at hearing voices and saw a group of men and women standing around the bed, then she must have slept again. When she woke up, it was three days after the car her father had been driving had gone off the road and crashed into a telephone pole and she, the sole passenger, was thrown a hundred yards away onto the five-foot way.

"So, you finally woke up," the neat little nurse said, pushing

61

before her a white enamelled cart loaded with vials, bottles, rolls of cotton wool and gauze, metal cups, sponges, trays of syringes, scissors, knives, and other gleaming steel utensils. "We're going to clean you up today. Your bandages need a changing." Out came a large pair of scissors. Snipping deftly she dropped masses of gauze into a plastic pail. The gauze was clean, then stained with yellow ointment, then brown with dried blood. The last layers were stuck to the body and whenever the nurse peeled a piece, it left the wound freshly raw and bleeding. It took an hour to peel the dried gauze off and Su Weng, exhausted, had stopped screaming by then. It was apparent there wasn't much whole skin left on her. The nurse was sweating and trembling as she washed Su Weng with a cool liquid and re-applied the ointment; this time, only a light gauze was taped.

"Eh, you can hear ten miles away. People think you're being murdered, lah! You got a lot of pain?"

The dim grey shape shifted, focussed, and coalesced. Su Weng stared numbly at the woman who was surveying her, it seemed, in close-up.

"You're in Ward 4B. My name is Fadzillah Hashim, I been in 4B for one month already, so, you wanna know anything, just ask me. Must have fun in this place, you know. Otherwise can die, lah!" She giggled and hopped on one foot. Su Weng became aware that the giddy motion of Mrs Hashim's shape was not just because of her own dizziness but because Mrs Hashim was constantly fidgeting. She was in a continuous dance and the white hospital gown swayed and bobbed as her head and shoulders weaved and her arms swung. "You come and see me in room 10. I know everybody in 4B. Can introduce you to some nice boys. You're not so bad. Cannot see your face anyway, so doesn't matter if you're not pretty, eh?"

"Mrs Hashim, Mrs Hashim, visitors for you," the call came from somewhere. She ducked around the screen and Su Weng found herself alone and finally wide awake.

Loud confident voices were walking along the corridor outside her room. Concealed by the screen, a patient groaned to the right. A nurse came and removed the left screen; the bed on the left which was by the door was empty. Su Weng gazed eagerly out through the open door.

Her mother and brother came. He sat on the metal folding chair next to the bed and said nothing. Her mother stood by the side and explained that her father had not been hurt in the crash, but he would not be able to visit because hospital sights and smells upset him. Su Weng's eyes filled with tears. She was her father's pet, and she knew he must be distressed by the accident.

A clatter and heavy smell of boiled vegetables and rice reminded them that it was dinner time. Her mother waited to see the kind of food served to Su Weng: watery potato soup, a bowl of rice, a plate of pale cabbage, and a saucer of stringy beef. "I will bring liver and spinach tomorrow. Hospital food isn't nutritious. You must promise not to eat anything with soy sauce in it. Soy sauce will scar and blacken your wounds." Su Weng thought of the numerous stitches on her face, arms, legs, and back, and of the white and pink flesh that the nurse had stripped, and she nodded.

She was studying dismally the rejected tray of food which her mother had left on the chair when Mrs Hashim appeared at the door. "Visitors gone? Nuisance, eh? Always make you feel bad. Never mind, I'll get a nicer visitor for you." She disappeared and returned a few minutes later pulling a young man along beside her. "This is my friend, Chun Hong. He's a very bright boy, in university in Australia. But cannot take the pressure, eh, Chun Hong? Come back home because got stomach ache all the time."

"Actually, I have ulcers," he said.

"Really cute, eh? Like elephant nose," Mrs Hashim said, waving her hand at the thin plastic tube which was clipped into his right nostril and which dangled down his pyjama shirt.

"I can't eat solids. This tube drips liquids into my system." His face was sallow and melancholy; thick black hair sprang, uncombed, straight up from his forehead. His expression of reluctance and embarrassment changed to curiosity. "I heard you had a concussion. Do you remember anything about the accident?"

Su Weng shook her head.

"Nothing about coming to the hospital? Perhaps you're better off not remembering. Mrs Hashim has been telling me all sorts of things about you. You're on your way to the university in Kuala Lumpur."

 Su Weng nodded and began to cry. She was supposed to have left for the campus in a week when the car went off the road. Now she wouldn't be there for the beginning of the first term.

"Hey, hey, no crying allowed here!" Mrs Hashim said with a

wild jump. She did a little dance. "Tomorrow you ask the nurse if you can get up and we'll have a party. Chun Hong and I must visit other people now." She grabbed his hand and pulled him out of the room. He smiled and winked as he left.

Su Weng stopped crying immediately. Her left foot was hot and throbbing; she tried to sleep, but the pain flashed every few seconds like the beam of a lighthouse sweeping through a dark ocean swell. When the nurse came to give her medication, she swallowed a sleeping pill and slept fitfully. Now and again she woke and listened to the woman in the next bed moaning. The fluorescent lights outside cast a pale glow in the room. Half asleep through the night she heard the nurses' murmurs as they passed each other and their footsteps hurrying up and down the long corridor.

The next morning, as the nurse changed her bandages, she gripped her pillow hard and didn't scream. The gauze came off more easily this time, and, besides, she knew that somewhere, Mrs Hashim was listening. "No, you can't get out of bed," the nurse said as she turned her over and slipped a fresh sheet under her. "You can't put your foot down yet. The doctor thinks you may have blood poisoning." The cut on the left foot had left the white bone showing, the nurse explained, and even with twenty-two stitches, if the infection got out of control, she might lose the foot. After the nurse had tucked the grey blanket in and bundled the soiled linen out of the room, Su Weng sat up in bed and reached over and touched her bandaged foot. It had ballooned to twice its normal size.

"Must stay in bed, eh? Never mind. Your foot won't drop off," Mrs Hashim said. Su Weng blinked back her tears. "You know how to play poker? I got cards here." Mrs Hashim waved a pack of worn pink-backed cards. "No money involved. Cannot gamble, you know, but just for fun, eh. We pass the time like good friends." She perched on the bed and dangled her slippers with her toes. Swiftly she dealt and laid the cards on the uncrumpled sheet. Su Weng picked them up painfully; her right hand was taped up and only her fingers were free to manoeuvre. They played for a while, Su Weng silent and Mrs Hashim laughing and calling out in excitement. "*Ada nasib!*" she exclaimed as she won a hand. "Oh, oh, dangerous, lah! Must watch out for you!"

"Mrs Hashim, Mrs Hashim, where are you?"

"Sshhh." She put a finger to her lips.

64

"Mrs Hashim," the nurse said, standing at the door with her hands on her hips. "You know you're not supposed to be out of bed. Doctor's orders. CRIB, remember!" Mrs Hashim picked up her cards and waved them unpenitently. "You must stop disturbing the patients."

"She wasn't disturbing me," Su Weng protested, waving back with her left hand.

"She's probably got you over-excited, your temperature's gone up," the nurse said, putting her hand to Su Weng's forehead. "Lie back and go to sleep."

"What is CRIB?"

"Doctor's orders for Mrs Hashim. Complete Rest In Bed. She's not supposed to get out of bed at all. The same for you." She frowned down and left.

Mrs Hashim was back many times and the nurses' cries of "Mrs Hashim, CRIB!" became commonplace to Su Weng. In a week her foot had healed enough for her to hobble to the bathroom down the corridor. "Eh, you," Mrs Hashim said as Su Weng emerged, damp and flushed from a tortured shower. "Come and meet Uncle Tan." She took Su Weng's towel and dripping soapbox in one hand and supported her at the elbow with the other. Dancing and hobbling, they walked down the length of the dormitory-style second-class area. It was a section for patients undergoing surgery. In some beds men and women slept like grey stones; in others, they were reading or gazing ahead of them or sitting by the sides of the beds bent over. Mrs Hashim stopped by a bed; a heavy man in his fifties was sitting up in it, propped on his pillow and reading *The Straits Times*. He was wearing the usual hospital pyjamas for men, a grey and white-striped shirt and trousers, and he had his legs stretched out with the ankles crossed. From his neck downward he appeared massive and inert, but when he looked up, his brown face flashed with life and intelligence. His smile lifted his eyebrows and crinkled the skin around his eyes.

"Aha, Mrs Hashim! Have you come to cheer me up?"

"Oh, Uncle Tan, you are the one with the good jokes. This is my friend, Su Weng. Under the bandages she is a pretty woman." They laughed while Su Weng smiled bitterly. "Uncle Tan is a very smart man," Mrs Hashim said, taking Su Weng by the hand and guiding her to the bedside. "He's a philosopher, you know, a lover of wisdom. Uncle Tan's been married, eh?"

"Two wives," he replied. "Two big mistakes."

"Don't say that," Mrs Hashim exclaimed. "Mrs Tan will be very sad to hear that."

"In the first marriage, my wife was the mistake, but now, I am the mistake," he responded.

"Come, come, Uncle, a clever man like you! You are a big prize for any woman."

"Ah, yes, an expensive prize, and Mrs Tan is a poor woman. So, have you come to wish me good luck?"

"*Nasib*, you're asking me for *nasib*? Cannot, lah, Uncle, I got too little. What you want good luck for?"

"I'm going for the operation on Wednesday. You think I will come out all right?"

"Very hard to kill a big man like you. You come out of the operation with less, but don't worry, your wife won't miss what the doctor take away."

Mr Tan looked suddenly very sad. "I don't know . . ." he sighed as if he were tired.

Mrs Hashim rose up quickly from the bed. "Must leave you, eh. You need rest for the big day. Cheer up, Uncle." She was bobbing down the long room before Su Weng could gather her towel and soapbox to leave.

Mr Tan had closed his eyes; his face was now a grey mass of wrinkles and unhappy droops, and Su Weng limped away without saying goodbye.

Su Weng had few visitors; her friends had left already for the start of the term in the university. The patches of flesh from where the skin had been torn away were healing slowly. By the second week, only her mother came to visit regularly. Every evening she brought a triple tiffin carrier, the lowest dish filled with rice, the second with fried liver, and the top dish with watercress soup. The blood lost, she said, was best replaced by eating the freshest pork liver, and the shock to Su Weng's spirit which was causing her to droop her head and cry each evening was best treated by a potion of bitter bark and ginger steeped in rice-wine and masked by sprigs of watercress. She would get up to leave only after Su Weng had eaten a satisfactory meal. Su Weng thought the tears which involuntarily rolled down her cheeks every evening were caused actually by her strong distaste for the slices of grey liver and the pungent soup, but she concentrated on her mother's hope for her recovery and swallowed each spoonful silently.

One evening, her mother had to attend a relative's funeral and Su Weng was alone during the dinner hour. Rejecting the hospital meal, she decided to see what Mrs Hashim was eating on her Muslim diet. As she approached Mrs Hashim's first-class room, she heard a loud chatter of many voices. Around Mrs Hashim's bed were clustered a number of women dressed in bright *baju kurongs*; on the bed with her, children were lying, some clinging to her arms and some sprawled by her feet. By the window sat an old woman with a baby on her lap. A handsome man stood by the head of her bed observing the activities with a broad smile.

"Eh, my friend, Su Weng. *Mari-lah*, and meet my family."

Su Weng stood shyly by the door, conscious of the coarse faded gown in which she felt like an abandoned orphan. Mrs Hashim was also dressed in a similar gown, but, surrounded by children, she appeared like a mother goddess robed in flowing white.

"These are my children, Ibrahim, Ahmad, Norina, Nazir." She tapped them gently on their heads as she named them, and they each adoringly tried to capture her swiftly moving hand. "And there is my youngest, Fatimah," she said, gesturing toward the elderly woman by the window. "And my mother-in-law."

"*Masok*, lah," the woman smiled, showing her toothless gums, and the baby stared at Su Weng with round solemn eyes.

"My sisters and sisters-in-law," Mrs Hashim continued, motioning toward the women who (with the same solemn gaze as the baby's) had all stepped back to observe Su Weng. "And my husband, Abdul Hashim."

The man shook her hand courteously, said in an indifferent tone, "How do you do?" and turned back to his wife. The women began chattering again and the children tugged at Mrs Hashim possessively with cries for attention. Su Weng waved good-bye to the mother-in-law who was still smiling sweetly at her and walked away; there was clearly no room for her in there.

"Do you know Mrs Hashim has five children?" Su Weng asked Chun Hong. They were standing by an open window along the corridor watching the cars and vans drive up the hill on which their building was situated. When they tired of visiting each others' rooms

67

or playing cards or reading, they would stroll down the corridor and lean over the windows to look enviously down on the traffic and pedestrians hurrying below, seemingly full of purpose and health. Chun Hong no longer carried the tubes attached to his body and he would be leaving in a week if his ulcers had healed by then.

"Why are you surprised?"

"Well, I never thought of her having a family outside."

"Don't you have a family outside?"

"What do you mean?" Su Weng was offended.

"You're angry," he repeated calmly. "Do you think I have a family?"

"I don't know. I suppose so. Everyone has a family somewhere."

"Most people do. It depends on what you think is a family. I used to think I didn't have a family. I read too many Western books. When I went to Adelaide, I discovered what family was. Actually, the reason I got so sick there was that I was depressed for a long time. I was lonely in Australia. The moment I got home, I felt better. I'm not close to my parents, you know. They're Chinese-educated, have a bicycle shop in Tampines, but with a family, you take what you have. I don't ask to be different from them any more." Chun Hong spoke slowly. There was a suggestion of sadness in his voice. "But you haven't decided what you want to be yet. You are still in conflict." He held her hand diffidently. Su Weng felt sorry for him.

Mrs Hashim found them playing cards that afternoon. "Sshhh," she whispered. "I'm CRIB. Come, I've found a secret place." They walked through the ward in which every bed seemed inhabited by a prone figure suspended between lunch and tea-time. They passed the first-class section, through a heavy fire-door, into a large room with windows on three sides, cushioned rattan chairs, lounges, and low book-cases. "This is the doctors' rest room," Mrs Hashim said with a throaty laugh. "But no doctors come, lah. So far, always empty. We can talk here till tea-time."

"How did you meet your husband?" Su Weng asked. His broad handsome face and good eyes still intrigued her.

"Ah, another woman interested in Mr Abdul Hashim!" Mrs Hashim replied in a sarcastic manner. "We met in college. He was a *kampong* boy, never dated until he met me. I was an Arts Freshie, he was a senior in Engineering. We got married the next year because he was going to Manchester to study."

Su Weng was confused. "You went to England?"

"Oh, yes. What's so wonderful about England? Just another country." Mrs Hashim's voice softened. "Three years in Manchester. No children yet, no mother-in-law, no sisters-in-law, Abdul has a heart. We went to London a lot, lots of trips, parties." She began to bounce lightly in her seat. "That was a long time ago. Now Abdul is head of the Municipal Waterworks, very important job." She began to speak in pidgin, tripping the words like a simple melody. "Life funny, eh? Now I'm Mrs Hashim. Yah, the doctor say I stay two more weeks here. Must watch my blood count."

"I'll visit you," Chun Hong said. *— makes it a*

"Oh, you visit your girlfriend, eh, Su Weng?" *question-lah*

But Su Weng had taken a *Readers' Digest* Condensed Books *makes* volume from the shelf and pretended not to hear. *it an exclam*

It was Friday, eleven A.M., a time when orderlies, nurses, and doctors had completed their morning duties and the men and women in Ward 4B, bandaged, medicated, and tranquillized, were left alone amid the sharp ammonia scent of mopped floors to contemplate time passing before the clatter of lunch carts and the smells of food, like the smells of wet clothes steaming before a fire, announced that time had, indeed, passed. Mrs Hashim took Su Weng to visit Mr Tan who had an emergency operation that morning, two days after surgery for a hernia. His bed was screened all around and in the shadowed quiet of the small enclosed womb, Mr Tan was lying motionless. They stood silently observing him sleep. His face was drawn and quite peaceful. Then he opened his eyes and looked at Mrs Hashim. For a moment, a recognition flickered in his eyes.

"Uncle, *ada baik*?" Mrs Hashim leaned over and spoke softly with her face close to his. "We missed you, eh. Where you been?"

Mr Tan said distinctly in a hoarse whisper, "In another country." He moved his hand as if to reach for her and closed his eyes.

Mrs Hashim leaned by his side for another moment while his eyes remained closed. Then she walked away without her usual dancing motions and went to her room to lie down.

Chun Hong visited Su Weng on Monday morning to say goodbye. Dressed in a white shirt and khaki pants he looked ordinary and

69

dull. Only the pallor of his complexion and his long uncut hair indicated that he had been ill for some time. "I'll ring you when you come for the holidays," he said as he shook her hand.

"Aren't you coming back to visit Mrs Hashim?"

"No, there's no point."

"No point? I don't understand." Su Weng felt a shock of anger. Her face was sullen as she stepped back and sat on her bed.

"You like Mrs Hashim," he responded, his thin face unmoved and still friendly.

"Yes, she's the happiest person in the ward."

He shook his head. "If being crazy is happy, she's happy."

"She isn't crazy!" Su Weng said violently. "She just can't stay still."

"She's a manic-depressive." He began to walk up and down by her bed, turning occasionally to give her a quick look. "Besides, she's never going to get well. She has leukemia."

Su Weng pressed her fingers into her palms. Her eyes were pricking with tears and she stared at him hatefully. She didn't want to hear what Chun Hong was saying.

"You don't know what these words mean, do you?" he asked.

Su Weng could only repeat, "She's not crazy."

He stopped pacing and took her tightly fisted hand. "We're all crazy. I'm crazy; I'm depressed all the time. Mr Tan is crazy; he's dying and doesn't know where he is. You're crazy also, but don't know it." He said all this calmly as if he were instructing her.

She remained silent and allowed her hand to remain in his.

"It's different here. Things are normal here that are crazy outside. When you return home, you'll find that you've changed. You won't be normal anymore."

Su Weng didn't believe him, but she didn't wish to argue. "All right." She pulled her hand gently away from his grip. "I hope you'll be okay in the future."

He suddenly appeared embarrassed, mumbled some words, and left abruptly.

She stayed in her room the rest of the day, reading and waiting for her mother's visit. Mrs Hashim didn't appear. On Tuesday, she went to look for Mrs Hashim and found that she had been moved to the isolation room at the end of the ward and wasn't permitted any visitors except for her family. Su Weng was leaving the ward the next day; she had already missed two weeks of study in the university.

Before she changed out of the hospital gown into the dress that her mother had brought, Su Weng sneaked into the isolation room to say good-bye. Mrs Hashim was sitting up in bed reading a Penguin paperback on art in the Muslim world. She had grown perceptibly thinner in the last few days, but she gave a gleeful grin when Su Weng slipped through the door. "Getting lonely, eh? What to do! Nurses make sure I stay in bed all the time."

"I'm leaving today, Mrs Hashim," Su Weng said, drawing nearer.

Mrs Hashim's eyes were full of grieving. "So soon going away? Good luck, eh. You looking beautiful today." *has the stranger accent — related to her craziness*

Su Weng felt her mouth dry up; she thought she had never loved a friend like Mrs Hashim, but she didn't know what to say. "I hope you'll be all right," she whispered.

"Oh, fine, fine, I'm doing fine. The doctors say, maybe two more weeks, then I can go home also." Mrs Hashim had dropped her book and was waving her hands elaborately. She jiggled up and down as if impatient and the metal bars on the bed creaked.

"Oh, Mrs Hashim," Su Weng exclaimed, alarmed, "complete rest in bed, remember! Please don't get excited. Good-bye!" and she left hastily, vigorously waving good-bye.

Walking down the hill with her mother, Su Weng turned back and looked up toward the windows of Ward 4B. She wondered which was the window that Chun Hong and she had leaned over these past three weeks envying the people wandering below. Someone was leaning out of a window on the fourth floor, and, for a moment, she thought she recognised Mrs Hashim's face, but, of course, it was too far off for her to be sure. Briefly she pondered on the misery in Mrs Hashim's eyes earlier, then she looked up at the trees which lined the hospital road and at the great green stars springing from their branches, and she felt a tremendous happiness at being alive.

Sail Boat

Lim Thean Soo

Reliving the past by crossing the bridge of time back four decades requires tremendous mental effort on our part. There is resistance when the memory, jaded by the daily grind, is deliberately jogged. The result of the attempt is a disconnected hodge-podge, disjointed fragments, a frustrating failure. Occasionally, however, the past returns to us compellingly and with vivid clarity as if the event that happened and our involvement in it were only a night's sleep away. Yes, the past does come back to us voluntarily, reminding us not to forsake it, to impress on us the unity of living, that, after all, the conception of time is entirely in our mind. Under favourable circumstances, we can also evoke the past through our association with singular occurrences in our lives and with certain unique individuals who have crossed our lives. Our memory may be stimulated by a key event or related bits of a shattering experience involving thought, sense, and emotion, triggering off a chain reaction which brings back the past forcibly to us, whether we like it or not. Without warning, the past then overwhelms us and what we undergo can only be described as something transcendental or even spiritual. The trouble is that we cannot hold onto this spontaneous restoration long, but if we are creative writers, we could perhaps try to capture it in words as far as the limits of our craft can allow, perhaps making it a piece of art.

There I sat in the air-conditioned coach which was taking me along on an overseas holiday tour. Its windows were open and the aircon had been switched off. Outside it was sunny; the scene was a picturesque panorama of fjords, lakes, uplands, and forests. The gentle roll of the coach lulled me into nodding, and when it glided round a bend, the summer was on me, bright and burning. I stirred uncomfortably, took off my jacket, coaxed myself to take a nap, and dozed away, overcome by travel weariness. I was perspiring and started to feel clammy. I dreamt that the oppressive equatorial sun was beating down on me, almost singeing my hair and moustache. Although my eyes were closed, I could see the rubber trees along the highway, giving way to *lallang* and jungle shrub. I was returning to the village over the hill on a late afternoon but then I felt confused as the vehicle gave a big bump and I realised on awakening that I was not in a rural bus meandering its way along a winding track but in a coach with a cacophony of tourists. The tour guide, who had a fondness for telling stories of the hero Siegfried, requested us to shut all the windows because the driver wanted to turn on the aircon—it operated efficiently. Just before I woke up, I remembered that I had heard laughing and splashing in the cool crystal-clear water of an equatorial rural stream, afterward telling a somewhat austere-looking young man older than I to hand me a fishing net. Excitedly I shouted to him, "Sail Boat, quick pass me the net!" He looked at me with twinkling eyes and asked me, "What's the hurry? The prawn is held tightly in the loop." As he bent down, I noticed his face—strivingly mirthful, seemingly tranquil but inwardly serious. When I opened my eyes, the vision faded away. I was on one of those economy tours of Scandinavia. I looked out of the window. There were no rubber trees, *lallang*, or jungle shrub. There was no equatorial stream. Sail Boat was nowhere to be seen. The past had come instantly on me like that and disappeared in a wink. But it was not until after I had returned home by air after completing the tour that this past came thundering in to invade my privacy with vengeance and it happened on the night that my wife and children were away at a seaside resort.

I was just about to fall asleep when a storm tore across our city. Amidst the flashes of lightning that followed, I seemed to sense time slowing down until I was back forty years. It was that very day, less than a fortnight after war in our region had broken out, the global conflict that was to be known as the Second World War, and whether the name was an allusion to man's neurotic adventurism or his immutable imbecility, I cannot say. At that time, I had reflected that maybe there need be no world war; if, as Mencken had put it, babies came into the world with larger cerebrums and smaller adrenal glands. Anyway, the Western democracies were ill-prepared for it;

moreover, their peoples seemed to have forgotten Vegetius' maxim that those who desired peace should prepare for war. Yes, I relived that day when our town was bombed and the sequential events came crashing down on me, as if they were run off a glass screen from a videotape recorder. Forty years ago, the announcement of war caught all of us in a jingoistic frenzy. I remembered that my uncle was in masochistic rapture, haranguing me that in dangerous times people had to be committed, that they could not remain smug as protected subject people while England fought bitterly for survival, that the Allied powers were enmeshed in the most titanic struggle in history to smash the insidiously destructive forces of Fascism. Along the streets and in many clubs, there were raucous cries of chauvinistic antagonism against the foreign aggressor. Flags and banners were waved publicly; fists clenched and shook; fiery songs of loyalty reverberated. Defending guns and warplanes seemed to be more conspicuous than before. People talked of nothing but the war. Even the newspapers were caught in the emotional swell. The pervading patriotic sentiment, lifted up to a feverish pitch, had turned to hysteria and it would be our undoing, for we blindly believed in the capability of our defence and decried the military effectiveness of our antagonist. Surely the war would last only six months or so, we assured each other with cocksureness. Our side would win. The end of Fascist totalitarianism was in sight. We were so certain of that and we had to be cruelly shaken. The bubble burst overnight. Almost the whole course of war was altered when enemy aircraft sank the vaunted British warships in the sea off Kuantan. Gloom set in immediately. After that, the fortunes of the defenders changed dramatically and the news media churned out nothing but the withdrawal of the dispirited defending land forces to more secure positions.

Precisely at 11 A.M. on that fateful day, forty years back, everything changed in the town where I lived. I was at work in the municipal library preparing for its fastidious members a synopsis of twenty fiction books just purchased. Ironically one of them was *A Farewell to Arms*. My colleagues and I heard the distant drone of aeroplanes and the faint crack of anti-aircraft guns. The air raid siren started to wail in alternating high and low pitch as a peon ran to the office shouting excitedly that specks of aeroplanes could be seen approaching from the north. I was about to leave my desk when an elderly man, an avid reader, approached me and asked me when the twenty fiction books would be released for borrowing by members. He was rather deaf and I had to shout at him that this would be done in a week's time. I avoided further conversation with him and hurried to the window to join my colleagues. We could see nothing unusual except crowds thronging the street below and they were pointing to the sky behind our building. By now, the drone of planes was intense, like the rumbling of several steamrollers struggling along a road. I rushed down the staircase to the main road. I gazed upward. At a height of about 6,000 metres were twenty-seven silvery planes flying steadily in three inverted V-formations and not far behind them at a lower altitude were nine smaller planes in the same formation. An onlooker, a sprightly young man who was standing beside me, told me that the twenty-seven planes were bombers and the nine escorting them were fighters. All the planes seemed to show no interest in our town, for they bypassed it. A while later, however, the bigger planes swung around and started descending, all stylishly at a tilt. Disregarding with contempt the barking of the defending ack-acks, three of them released a batch of bombs. Another three came down at an angle and sent down a screaming flight of bombs; the others in threes successively despatched their lethal weapons. Explosions rent the air and they seemed to be louder and louder as the bombs continued to smash down. Not far away, to the east of our building, a spiral of dense dark smoke rose furiously to the sky while little patches of smoke could be spotted around the outskirts of our town. Nine bombers broke away from their companions and headed for the heart of the town. They unloaded all their bombs and so much smoke mushroomed up that the sun was temporarily occluded. The crowds shook their fists at the marauding planes as they disappeared into the clouds. The droning continued. All of a sudden, the onlookers began to cheer when they spotted three fighter planes emerging from the south and starting to chase the remaining eighteen bombers. These defence fighters were immediately set upon by the enemy escort fighters and a dogfight ensued. The crowds expected a drawn-out spectacle but it was all over within a few minutes. To their disappointment, compared to the adroit enemy fighters, the three defence planes were clumsy as buffaloes and they were all shot down. Some onlookers mistakenly assumed that the enemy fighters had been brought down and clapped their hands in glee. They quickly realised that they were wrong when the enemy fighters swooped down and started strafing our town. One of them hurtled down in the direction of the library and started to machine-gun it. Two persons on the street narrowly avoided the spray of bullets. People began to scurry for shelter and soon the streets were deserted. I dashed back to the library, scrambling up the stairs, and reached my desk. I could hear my heart pounding. The Head Librarian reprimanded me for leaving the office without permission and told me to seek shelter in the monsoon drain at the back of the building. As my colleagues and I scampered for safety, we heard the irritating whine of planes overhead and we inferred that the enemy bombers were bent on destroying our town's power station and their fighters in terrorizing the townsfolk by diving repeatedly down to shoot at them. We no longer heard the discharge of the defence ack-acks and assumed that they must have been bombed out. The bombers came down low. We suspected that they had come to finish us off and our hearts thumped wildly. We were tense, tired, and thirsty. Soon bombs rained down close to the library and the solid building shook to its very foundation, causing the ceiling, doors, and windows to rattle. The crash of bombs was so loud that instinctively I drew my hands to my ears. Several employees from nearby offices ran to our shelter and told us they had heard that our town was in shambles, the people panic-stricken. Law and order seemed to be on the verge of collapse. Looters had helped themselves to provisions in the unattended shops and markets. A young man narrated to us that he had telephoned home to find out if his family was safe but could not get the line through; he had learnt from a friend that several persons had already been killed in the air raid and there was no one to bury them. When the bombing ceased, the Head Librarian sent the peon to buy some food and drinks for the staff but the man returned to say that all the hawkers had disappeared and the coffee shops had put up their shutters. We crouched in the smelly monsoon drain until our limbs ached. We knew that the enemy planes had already gone away; yet the air raid siren had not sounded the all-clear. We were chafing at the delay when the siren gave out a long continuous blast. My colleagues and I sought permission from the Head to call it a day. We were worried that our homes might have been destroyed— nearly all of us in those days did not have telephones installed at our homes and we could not find out what had happened. Our boss instructed us to shut the library and go back. He had not been able to get a clear-cut directive as to whether the library should open the next day. He was very concerned about the books under his charge.

Our town bathed in golden light, a mix of smoke and sun; the smell of burning sulphur was strong. I cycled home with a sense of foreboding. The streets were almost empty, like those I saw in the Hollywood movies when the outlaws rode into town. There were no children in sight, not even in the back yards. The handful of visible inhabitants along the sidewalk were Air Raid Precaution staff and volunteers; solitary sentries stood on guard outside a few buildings and depots. I sensed that the townsfolk were in a state of apprehension. They concealed their feelings of unease behind closed doors and window shutters. I passed a music shop shut up for business and could not help reading its advertisement: "Arrived latest records. Carmen Miranda's *Chica Chica Boom Chic* and Betty Grable's *Two Hearts Met*." Funny that only ten days back they were selling like hot cakes! I turned round a bend and saw a roadblock ahead of me. Beyond this barrier, a fire was raging in a row of shophouses. A burly Air Raid Precaution official bawled at me, "Hey you, get away! Don't you know a war is on? Don't you realise that the enemy planes might return any time? Get away!" I was nonplussed but I understood that it was all a question of nerves. I made a detour and passed behind a deserted market. Someone in uniform gesticulated at me not to proceed further. He pointed to several partially destroyed houses in the distance; they were smouldering, with rubble piled around them. I dove into a back lane and headed for the residential area. As I crossed a junction, I noticed a small isolated crowd grimly watching a stretcher entering an ambulance. I stopped and got down from my bicycle. I was informed that a civilian had been struck by shrapnel. He was unfortunate, considering that all the occupants of the houses had fled before they were bombed. As soon as the ambulance left, the crowd vanished and I continued my solitary journey. The residential area appeared so lonely that I experienced an eerie feeling when I passed into it. Being reminded of a similar situation in one of H. G. Wells' novels about a journey back in time, I pedalled on furiously and did not look behind until I reached home by which time it was almost dark.

My uncle was at the gate to meet me. "Am I glad to see you safe and sound! Your aunt was worried to death about you!"

"Any news, First Uncle?"

"Get in and I'll tell you, Koon Giap."

Inside the house, my uncle briefed me about the situation. The invading army was only seventy kilometres away from our town. There remained only two white men working in the government hospital which was crowded with casualties. The defending troops, making their way south, looked exhausted and demoralised; they did not even seem keen in holding the town. In fact, fuel dumps and military stores were being destroyed. That was ominous. My uncle expected the invading army, making use of tanks, to capture our town within the next day or two. I expressed the hope that by some miracle the advance of the invaders would be stemmed. My uncle remarked that I, steeped in Herodotus and Szuma Chien, had been unduly influenced by accounts of the turn of events during wartime. Then, with a concerned look, he said, "Nephew, the situation's critical. You mustn't stay in this town. Auntie and I have decided so for your own good. You must leave early tomorrow morning for the village across the hill. I'll let you have the address of a friend who lives in an *attap* hut. You mustn't remain here. You'll be killed. The young people will be rounded up. Before your father died, I promised him that I would take care of you. So you must do as I've advised you. Don't worry about Auntie and me. We know how to take care of ourselves."

"Yes, First Uncle. Thank you for taking care of me all these years since I became an orphan."

I observed that his eyes were wet with tears as he murmured, "There's no time for sentiment. Go and pack your bag!"

My uncle was wrought. He must also have been disappointed by the deteriorating situation. Since yesterday, he had maintained a stony silence, breaking it only to mutter to himself, "Being a true blue isn't enough!" I understood—he had a British education and all his life he had been brought up believing in the invincibility of British arms. He had no children and he heaped his love on his library of English literature, a private collection second to none in our town. He never thought it possible that the world which he cherished so much would crumble before his eyes. He felt lost.

As soon as dawn peeped out of the horizon, I bade farewell to my uncle and aunt. Riding my bicycle I took the route across the hill well knowing that I might have to carry the machine over short stretches along the way. Nearing the foot of the hill, I was surprised to find that I had company; it seemed that, after the previous day's shattering air raid, some of the townsfolk were heading for the safety of the hill on the terraced slopes on which rested orchards of nutmeg and guava. It was disconcerting that the hill farmers reared so many fierce dogs who followed me tenaciously along the territories which they were supposed to guard. I had a tough time warding them off with my bicycle and stick. Only a month ago, I had read in the newspaper that the police had been combing the hill for subversive elements and spies. As I moved on, I sensed that the hill people were suspicious of strangers and I did not stop near their homes to take a rest. I reached the village just past noon.

After some time, I located the unnumbered hut where my uncle's friend, Mr Teo, lived. It was shut. According to the neighbour, he had gone to take his lunch. So I sat on the bench outside and ate the fried rice I had brought along. When Mr Teo came back, I quickly introduced myself to him and handed him my uncle's letter. He read it slowly and started scratching his head. There was, he told me, a problem because he was leaving for the south in a hurry. However, he would acquaint me with the Ung family—Mr and Mrs Ung, Mr Ung's mother, and the three Ung children. We followed a path along the riverbank upstream for nearly a kilometre and then turned left toward a house up on a slope. We entered the compound to the infernal din of barking dogs who rushed out to confront us. Mr Ung's bare-bodied second son dashed out to drive them away and he greeted Mr Teo.

"Is your father at home, Sail Cloth?" asked Mr Teo impatiently.

"Yes, he just came back from town. There was another air raid."

"This young man is Koon Giap, the nephew of a good friend of mine. I'm introducing him to your father."

I shook hands with Sail Cloth, a lithesome lad of fifteen years. He had a rustic look of honesty.

"Follow me, please! Don't worry about the dogs." The lad chased the dogs away and loped toward the house with boundless energy.

We struggled up a flight of steps to a large house bounded by a low wall with wooden planks above it and roofed with *attap*. Mr Ung came out to welcome us. He shook hands with Mr Teo and was soon huddled in a conversation with him. I saw Mr Ung nodding his head vigorously and he came up to where I sat talking to Sail Cloth.

"Koon Giap, you may stay with us as long as you like."

"Thanks, Ah Peh. I have some money with me. Please accept sixty dollars as an advance for my board and lodging."

"No, Koon Giap. On Mr Teo's recommendation, I have to give you shelter and food without payment. This is wartime."

"Please, Ah Peh. My uncle will be annoyed if I stay here at your expense."

"Nonsense! You're welcome! And may I ask how are your uncle and your aunt?"

"They're fine, thanks. About my lodging with you . . ."

Mr Teo did not let me finish what I had to say. He knew that my conscience was ill at ease and so he proposed to Mr Ung that the advance of sixty dollars be spent to buy rice, sugar, and provisions and I should keep the balance. Mr Ung would have none of it, but after some persuasion, he relented and accepted payment for only one bag of rice. At this stage, his comely wife and winsome daughter emerged from their room and he introduced them to me, telling them that he had accepted me as a guest. Out of politeness, I asked after their health. I then inquired from Mr Ung how his mother and elder son were.

"Oh, she's strong for her age. As for Sail Boat, he's well. This war has upset his career. You see, he used to teach Chinese in an English school and he's been told that all schools have been closed indefinitely. Sail Boat's too interested in world affairs. I've told him that it's better to be a farmer or a charcoal dealer like me but he . . ."

His wife interrupted him. "Koon Giap, we're indeed happy to have you with us. My daughter, Swee Lian, will prepare the bed for you. I hope you don't mind sleeping in the same room with Sail Cloth. We don't have an electricity supply in our house and I'm afraid that you've to get used to the mosquitos. We take simple food and I hope it will suit you." Swee Lian was smiling coyly at me and I caught her eye.

I could not sleep that night partly because it was warm and partly because I kept thinking about my uncle and aunt. I fanned away the mosquitos buzzing around my ears as best I could and felt restless. I could hear the nightjar's *kiuk kiuk* just before I fell asleep and it was already 3 A.M. by then.

I did not meet Sail Boat until late the next morning. I found him much older and taller than I. He had winning eyes and a firm lip. Intuitively I realised that he was a person of strong conviction and deep feeling. Because he had lost his teaching job, on the preceding day he had told his parents that he had gone to town to look for a temporary job. When his father introduced me to him, he shook my hands warmly. Even so, I felt that there was a distance between us which he tried to narrow. Apart from education, we were brought up differently and held dissimilar views. I knew that he regarded it odd that I should be a passive youthful bystander during wartime but he did not say it out loud. At any rate, he made his first attempt at a kindred bond with me when he proposed, "Koon Giap, it'd be dull for you to stay at home. I'm likely to be free for a day or two. Would you like to come prawn baiting with me?"

I welcomed it and nodded my head. Sail Cloth wanted to accompany us but his father directed him to help pack some of their belongings in case the war should spread to the village and they had to evacuate. It transpired that Sail Boat had informed his father that the invading army was only twenty kilometres from the town. This had caused his father to think about his own stepmother living in enemy-occupied territory in China. He had been supporting her for years by sending her money and foodstuffs but the extension of the war there had stopped that. Even though he felt depressed, he did not show it for he did not want to upset his elder son whose mind seemed to be engrossed with certain matters privy to him.

Mrs Ung fried *bee hoon* for us to bring along. I felt sorry for Sail Cloth who was not allowed to come along with us. Sail Boat carried a basket and a fishing net; he handed me a stick to ward off dogs. We walked a few kilometres before skirting a huge private estate. We then headed for a secluded bamboo grove beside the river. En route, Sail Boat had pointed out to me the place where I could have my daily bath, adding that the womenfolk washed their clothing and had their ablutions much farther downstream, a spot which the men avoided trespassing—years ago, a peeping tom who hid behind a rock was detected and beaten up by the villagers. Adjacent to the grove, the river water was still and its bed covered with scattered rocks. Sail Boat demonstrated to me how easy it was to catch the water snails, the flesh of which was to be used as bait.

He handed me two long ribs of *lidi* and told me to make a loop at each thin end. The loop of one *lidi* was to be tightened to hold the bait while the loop of the other was just big enough to slip through the tail of a prawn. The ploy, according to him, was to lure the prawn out of its hiding-place with the bait and use the loop to secure its body.

Sail Boat nudged me to watch how he did it. Expertly he let a prawn, resting in its seclusion, feed on a bit of the bait and slowly he drew it out from below the rock to the open. Using his right hand, he slipped the noose through the body of the prawn from under, jerked the *lidi*, and steadily pulled the struggling victim out of the water. He then pointed to the bottom of a boulder and whispered to me that a large prawn was hovering beneath it. I followed exactly what he had told me to do, but being inexperienced, I lost my first prawn in my hurry to get it to the surface and scoop it up with the fishing net. We were so absorbed in prawn catching that we hardly sensed the passage of time.

While I was counting the number of prawns captured, Sail Boat said to me, "I hear you're rather fond of books."

I smiled at him. "I can't help it because I work with them."

He suppressed a yawn and gave me a cryptic look. "The town library's too full of colonial books."

"I don't know about that." I saw no point in refuting him. John Gunther's *Inside Asia*, Tota Ishimaru's *Japan Must Fight Britain*, and many others on the shelves could hardly be labelled thus. At any rate, I could only infer what he meant by "colonial." I wondered why he had made that cussed remark. My silence made him realise that it had galled me and he tactfully changed the subject.

About an hour later, we heard the sound of distant gunfire. It was momentary but it woke us to the reality that war probably had reached the town. I prayed silently for uncle and aunt and wondered whether the invading army would destroy it. Sail Boat eyed me, reading what rankled in my mind. He suggested that we break off for lunch. I agreed, closing the basket almost half full of prawns. We sat down and quietly ate the *bee hoon* as sandflies hovered around us. We had hardly finished our meal when we heard the drone of aeroplanes overhead but they did not release any bombs. They were heading south.

"Did you enjoy catching the prawns?" Sail Boat's question drew me from thoughts about the war.

"Yes, very much indeed. It was kind of you to have taken me on this trip."

"Well, some other day Sail Cloth will accompany you to catch river fish and water frogs that are edible. I'm afraid I might be occupied in the next few days. You see, some of my pupils in town need my assistance during this critical period. We can't remain passive in this war."

I did not request him to explain what he meant by that. From what I had learnt of him from his younger brother, I surmised that Sail Boat together with his friends were willing to face danger and anonymously oppose the invaders. Was I right? Whether I was or not, I observed that Sail Boat suddenly became reticent and moody. When we reached home, he kept to himself.

The next morning, I helped Sail Boat and his brother to harvest three beds of groundnuts in the farm behind the house carved out from the hillside. We tilled the soil and manured the beds with chicken droppings. After lunch, the three of us climbed the hill scouring for firewood. We collected a large quantity and were making it into three bundles when we spotted Mr Ung approaching us. Out of breath, he stuttered, "Quick, get the firewood home! The town has fallen! At any moment, the invading troops might appear at the village. We must be ready to leave our home in case they do that."

When we reached the house, Sail Boat informed his father that he had to visit a few teacher friends in town. On hearing this, Mr Ung could hardly control his temper and he burst out, "That's what you always do. Meet your friends and maybe your pupils too. Meet them secretly. Don't you ever think of your parents and the old lady in these troubled times?"

Mrs Ung intervened and advised Sail Boat to go but he should be careful. She had heard that the town was full of enemy soldiers and had been told stories of their brash behaviour. Sentries shot at persons who did not bow to them. Sail Cloth complained quietly to me, "In the past few months, brother has been meeting his friends and other people. Whatever for? How can they fight an army of invaders? His duty is to this house. He's so touchy whenever our relatives remind him about it." His mother pulled him away, telling him to shut up. Swee Lian was standing at the corner looking unconcerned. I next noticed that she was fondly gazing at me. She had confided to me that she was determined to have a good education when the war was over and marry an educated man.

Later in the day, we heard that the invading troops had committed outrageous acts against young people and women. It alarmed us even though all sorts of rumours abounded. Carrying our personal belongings and food in home-made sacks, we left the Ung home for the hill where we slept uneasily for two nights in the open. On the third day, it began to drizzle and we felt miserable. We were concerned about the old lady, who could not stand the cold. Mr Ung made himself walk to the village for news and he learnt that the war had moved south. His friends told him that the town was still being guarded by enemy sentries but things were returning to normal. In the evening, we hiked downhill back to the Ung home. Swee Lian asked me when I would be going back to my town and I gave her a vague answer. After dinner, we found that the old lady was unwell. Out of courteous consideration, I postponed going to town to find out what had happened to my uncle and aunt.

On the following morning, Sail Boat slipped in while it was still dark. He appeared pale, haggard, and disturbed; his face was bruised on one side. I mentioned to him that his grandmother had fallen ill and he went into her room for a moment to have a look at her. When he came out, I asked him how he became bruised in the face.

"Shhh! I just saw Granny. She was sleeping, breathing heavily . . . About my face, my parents must not know. The *Kempeitai* and detectives were interrogating all young persons in town. They questioned me. I told them I was a coolie. They didn't believe me; examined my hands. They said I lied and beat me. I insisted I was a coolie. One of them bashed my face with a pistol butt. They let me go after recording my particulars. However, I never told them where I lived . . . I've come back to get some papers and my belongings. Don't tell my father what I've told you. Just say that I came here and had to go back to town in a hurry."

He entered his room and ransacked his cupboard. Before he left, he advised me, "Koon Giap, don't go to town. More enemy soldiers are marching in from the north. It's not safe for young people like you to be around. Please tender my apologies to my parents for not seeing them before I go. I'll be thankful if you could help Sail Cloth to look after them. Granny will recover. Please tell Swee Lian to attend to her needs. Good-bye!"

As soon as he walked out, bleary-eyed Sail Cloth came out from his bedroom and asked me where his brother had gone to. I replied that I did not know.

After breakfast, I informed Mr Ung that Sail Boat had returned home a while ago and hurriedly left. Mr Ung stared at me with a frown and knitted his eyebrows. "Gone back! Gone to plot with his friends? Gone looking for trouble? I fear he might involve us." I well understood why the old man had vented his anger at me and knew that he felt bad doing it.

The next day, I tried to seek Mr Ung's agreement for me to go back to my town but he would not listen to it. Instead he sent a man to find out how my uncle and aunt fared; after a few days, the man came back with the tidings that they were safe and sound. My uncle had forwarded a letter to me through him and I read it greedily. My uncle addressed me using my name initials. He went straight to the point. After experiencing the terror at the beginning of the enemy occupation, he and my aunt had settled down to the new situation. Our neighbour, the proprietor of a printing firm, had been taken away by the *Kempeitai* for questioning and had still not returned. All owners of wireless sets had to surrender them to the military on the pain of death. People were expressly forbidden to spread any rumours. They started to keep to themselves and became careful of what they said because overnight our town became thick with informers. Food was getting scarce and the prices of goods soared. It would be prudent for me not to return as yet. There was no work for me to do because the military had closed the town library. My uncle ended the letter by requesting me to burn it and I noticed that he had typed out the letter but not signed it.

To while away the time, I resorted to reading any book or magazine I could lay my hands on. Frequently I went out with Sail Cloth to catch prawns, fish, and frogs; en route, we visited the orchards of Mr Ung's friends. I taught Swee Lian how to read and write. She had never attended school before because her mother had not been able to cope with the work at home and on the farm. However, her father had grounded her in Mandarin. I observed that she was intelligent and learned fast. From her I found out why her father had named his sons Sail Boat and Sail Cloth. Her late grandfather used to be a *tongkang* captain. One day, Swee Lian mentioned to me that, should I return to my town, she would find ways and means to go and work there. Knowing that she had a sort of crush on me, I left it at that. I did not, of course, tell her that, just before war broke out, my aunt had been actively trying to arrange a marriage for me to someone else. The days passed by. Sail Boat did not return home and Mr Ung hinted to us that he did not wish his elder son's name ever to be mentioned in his presence. The old lady recovered and we felt more at ease.

Not long after, we were told that the military occupation authorities planned to stage a victory parade in my town on a Thursday, being exactly a month after it had been captured. The townsfolk would have liked to ignore the celebration but they were urged by their community leaders not to show any lack of enthusiasm for it. When the day arrived, the procession comprising a leading platoon of enemy soldiers, occupation administrators and selected staff, reluctant civilian representatives, two *chingay* groups, local bands, and drivers of floats assembled at the town square. The procession was guarded by the *Kempeitai*, plainclothes men, and policemen. Immediately after the firing of crackers aloft a pole, it started to move. The crowd watching the parade was small; few people bothered to wait along the route of the procession to see it pass by. It had hardly moved forward half a kilometre when loud explosions and piercing screams were heard. Smoke could be seen emitting from the front of the parade, which broke up in confusion. Bodies lay lifeless on the road. The military authorities were very annoyed at the outrage which caused the death of two soldiers, a member of the *Kempeitai*, and three civilian participants, besides injuring several bystanders. From the grapevine, we soon learnt that two young males had lobbed hand grenades at the head of the procession and made good their escape in the ensuing confusion. One of the attackers had his hand blown off when a hand grenade exploded prematurely. He was helped away behind a motorcycle and blood dripped along the road. The soldiers opened fire at them but to no avail. Pamphlets advocating resistance against the fascist aggressor were found scattered along the roadside.

The morning newspaper provided only a skimpy account of the daring attack and added that the military authorities would soon apprehend the culprits. Raids on suspected premises in our town and the adjoining areas were conducted; large numbers of young persons were roped in for brutal interrogation. Because of this, Mr Ung warned me not to go back to town. However, I was beginning to feel bored staying in his house enjoying his hospitality. At noon, someone hollered at the gate for me and the dogs started their infernal din. Sail Cloth went to where I was chopping firewood and told me that a male stranger wanted to see me urgently and privately. I presumed that he must have brought news for me from my uncle and I hurried to meet him while Sail Cloth chased away the dogs.

The man, tall and unshaven, addressed me grimly, "You're Koon Giap?"

"Yes!"

"How would I know?"

I glared at him. When he repeated his question, I did not conceal my annoyance and raised my voice, "I'm Koon Giap. Who the bloody hell are you? What do you want?"

"Not so loud, young man. You're a friend of Sail Boat?"

"Yes, but . . ."

"You mustn't tell anyone, not even his parents. He's seriously wounded. He wants help at once!"

"What happened? Where is he?"

"His right hand's been severed. An accident, Koon Giap. But no one must know, especially after yesterday's incident."

I gasped. Hastily I put two and two together. Sail Boat must have been the person whose hand had been blown to bits by the hand grenade. The explosion would also have affected his already bruised face and body as well—so I imagined. He required immediate medical attention. The *Kempeitai* would be looking for him. His mother would die of grief if she came to know about this.

"What can I do to help him?" I noticed Sail Cloth peering at us from a distance.

The man eyed me slyly. "I know your type. You don't want to be involved if you can't help it. But once you're in it, you'll never back out. I know you'd help us. This is a matter of life and death. Not only for Sail Boat's sake. Other people are in it. Their lives are at stake. Complete secrecy is required."

"Yes, yes! I know that!" My voice sounded impatient.

"Right! I want you to help me get anti-tetanus and morphine injections. But not from the doctors. All clinics and dispensaries are under close watch."

"I know a pharmacist friend in my town. He might have it. I'll bring you to see him. I'll inform Mr Ung that I'm going to town to see my aunt because she wants my help to open a foodstall. That will be a good excuse. In fact, I'm dying to go home."

"There's no more time to waste. Go and tell Mr Ung. Make some excuse that it's urgent. Say I'm busy. We've to go to town straightaway."

I ran in and collected my belongings. I took leave of the Ungs. Sail Cloth felt sad while Swee Lian looked at me as if to ask me whether I would ever return. She had heard that I had given my bicycle to Sail Cloth.

I joined the man at the gate. We walked briskly to catch the ramshackle village bus. While we were waiting for the bus to move, I asked the man what I should tell my pharmacist friend if he were to inquire who wanted the injections. The man immersed himself in deep thought.

"Don't worry. I'll give him a name and an address. And if your friend should check up, he'll find someone there with a maimed foot. I'll have that arranged and I've to act fast."

I did not press him for further details as the bus had begun to move. After a tedious ride, we reached town in the evening. I was glad to see my home town again. I observed that the *Kempeitai* and the police were busy searching bus passengers. We were allowed to proceed after a check. The town was scarred with bombed-out houses and scattered debris. There were no enemy soldiers in sight as they had all moved south. Arriving at my friend's residence, I let my companion spin his story about his brother having stepped on a rusty nail. No doctor dared to visit his brother because he lived in a secluded place and there was difficulty in arranging transport to fetch his brother to town. I kept a straight face and had to assure my friend that it was true. I noticed that he was uneasy and he mentioned to us the hand grenade outrage which had occurred on the preceding day. I sidestepped that and instead asked him whether he had the two types of injection. He nodded his head. Apparently he had taken some medicine from his dispensary for safe-keeping at home, partly because he feared that it would be requisitioned by the military authorities and partly because he wanted to sell it surreptitiously in the black market. However, he could not make up his mind to let us have what we wanted. My friend's mother watched us pleading to her son; she intervened and told him to relent. After what seemed to have been an interminable lapse of time, my friend reluctantly agreed to let us have the injections, enjoining us not to tell anyone about the sale. He handed over the medicine, including a bottle of M&B 693 which he strongly recommended to us, in a bundle to my companion who promptly paid him. We promised my friend to keep the matter secret, and left. We took the bus back to the village. I much regretted that I was still unable to call on my uncle and aunt. When we arrived at the bus terminus, we were surprised to find the police conducting a search of all passengers and their effects. My companion handed the parcel to me and told me in a whisper to pass it back to him at the rear window after he had been searched. He then edged forward to be among the first to be checked. I saw him subjecting himself for examination. On board the bus, I was quaking with fear—I was the last person queuing in the rear when I spotted his upraised hands just above a window and stealthily handed the parcel to their care. I did it in the nick of time and I felt almost certain that no one saw me doing it—there was a timely distraction when a bus entering the terminus crashed headlong into a stationary motor car. After this, I quickly followed behind the last but one passenger about to step down from our bus. The police observed that I was flustered and made me undergo a thorough body check but they found nothing and released me. I joined my companion in the change-over bus but was careful not to sit beside him. I noticed that he had kept the parcel below the corner seat where he was sitting. He looked cool and composed.

After a ride lasting an hour, we got off the bus at the entrance to a lonely estate. It was already dark. A stranger on a bicycle waved at us from beside a clump of bushes and we hurried toward him. My companion did not find it necessary to introduce him to me. The stranger took the parcel from my companion and gruffly told us to follow him. We walked at a fast pace and reached a dimly-lit hut from where I could hear muffled moaning. I saw Sail Boat stumbling toward us. I felt that it must have hurt him badly to come out like that to greet me. In an agitated voice, I asked him if his right hand still hurt and why he was not resting.

"Koon Giap, I have to say this. Both my hands are unhurt. It's my comrade's right hand which has been blown off. He's now lying in bed inside. He's a brave man. . . . Koon Giap, I'm sorry to have deceived you. There was no other way to get you to help my injured friend. If our messenger, the man we sent to Mr Ung's house, hadn't told you that my right hand had been severed, you wouldn't have gone out of your way to help us. Please forgive me. At any rate, we all here wish to thank you for what you've done for us."

I looked hard at Sail Boat. Even in the dim light, I could make out that his eyes were frigid and I saw the flicker of a fanatical glint. His lips were firmly pressed together. All of a sudden, I felt very angry that I had been made use of even though I understood why he had to resort to subterfuge. For many seconds, I could not say anything as he continued, "You'll have to leave us after dinner. The man who brought you here will escort you back to your village. You can't stay here. It's too risky. We've to depend on you to hold your tongue!"

I had been involved. I had already done a favour to Sail Boat. Now I could retire, return to my uncle and aunt. Right then, I could not help mulling over what Sail Boat and the man had really achieved. The cynic in me told me that what they had done would not influence the course of the war or their cause one jot. I could not help comparing Sail Boat with Sung Chiang in Shih Nai-an's novel, *The Water Margin*. His exploits would likely imperil people caught in the maelstrom of counter-espionage and anti-resistance. Was Sail Boat, in emulating Wen Tien-hsiang, blinded by patriotic zeal or was he selfishly trying to satisfy his ego? Did he think that he was a hero? Like Yo Fei who fought the Kin? I felt like kicking myself for having acceded to Sail Boat's messenger, for having been taken in. I had studied European history and knew that nations could be enemies one day and friends the next—one day it could be the Battle of Waterloo and another the Marne. And alliances have changed constantly. . . . Outside the hut, the wind was starting to rustle the leaves and the lightning streaks lit the horizon. Suddenly I felt cold and a sense of emptiness overwhelmed me. . . . The storm in the city had abated. I tossed over to the other side and tried to sleep in the bedroom of my apartment. Forty years back in time seemed like yesterday. I could not help reflecting on the mission of Robert Jordan to blow up the bridge as I continued to think about Sail Boat. The temple bells had already sounded the knell for Sail Boat as those in the church would one day toll for me. And I looked at the corner of the bookcase where I had kept Hemingway's novel side by side with an English translation of *The Chronicle of Ōnin*.

Out of the Storm

Woo Keng Thye

He sat motionless looking out of the window of the hut. Outside the storm showed no sign of abating. This was the third day of the storm.

Blasts of cold wind tore at the hut threatening to blow off the *attap* roof. The man was trembling from the cold and his joints would have stiffened if not for the thick jacket he was wearing. All that he could discern of the once green countryside was now a vast expanse of muddy flood waters.

Lightning had struck at several tall trees and even as he watched, another flash of lightning was followed by a fresh peal of thunder. Between the constant patter of raindrops he could hear the gushing of currents of water. Finally, he turned his eyes to the fire which was dying out. In a little while, only the red hot glow of the embers would remain.

He was about to rekindle the fire when he thought he heard a knock on the door, but on reflection, he decided it was more likely the rattling of the door due to the strong winds. He stoked up the fire and somehow felt more at ease with the fire glowing strongly. Then he heard the knock again. It was more distinct.

Cautiously he went to the door which he had latched. He hesitated for what seemed a long time, afraid of what he might find outside on a dark stormy evening. Against his better judgement he finally opened the door. The wind tore at him and the rain beat against him. But simultaneously, he noticed somebody slumped on the ground just beyond the door.

It was an unconscious woman. With an effort, he lifted her into his bed. Quickly he shut the door to keep out the wind and rain.

Gently he eased her out of the slicker that she was wearing and in the process he realised that she was running a high fever. At the same time he noticed that parts of her clothing were torn as if she had had a struggle and someone had ripped them. It was then that he saw the patch of blood on the sheet.

He had to stop the bleeding from her thigh. Quickly, he tore a strip off one of his clean shirts and pressed it against the raw wound. After a while, the bleeding stopped. He cleansed her wound with some boiled water and applied a crude dressing to it.

She was moaning while he was cleaning the wound but she did not put up a struggle. Her breathing had become less rapid and more regular, and the colour had returned to her face.

She was young, barely eighteen years old. Her hair was long and jet black. Her features were a combination of Indian and Chinese which explained her brown complexion.

In repose she had a certain comeliness. She was about five and a half feet tall and slim.

He applied a cold towel to her forehead and just as he stood up she opened her eyes, and let out a wild shriek and attacked him. She clawed him and bit into his arms.

He was unprepared for the sudden attack. Immediately he thought of the blanket. Shaking it open he managed to wrap her in it and held her down, but as suddenly as the attack had come, she was quiet again. Her eyes closed and she went to sleep. He realised that she must have had a nightmare, probably reliving a nasty experience.

He boiled some porridge and added some slivers of dried fish, bits of garlic, and a couple of tomatoes. Fortunately, he had harvested his green garden at the back of the house before the storm as most of it would have been uprooted and swept away by the heavy rain.

He had not realised until now that the rain was showing signs of abating. Outside the night was pitch dark. The steady pitter-pat on the *attap* roof was like somebody beating on a drum. If the rain stopped the next day he would go out and catch a couple of water-fowl or at least some fish from the pond. In a few days' time when the water had receded and the sun was shining brightly again, he would till the land and plant the next crop of *padi*.

Her sudden groan jolted him out of his reverie. The broth was ready. He would try waking her up for a bit of it.

Going up to her, he gently unwound the blanket around her. The fever seemed to have subsided but her face was still flushed. He shook her gently but there was no response from her. Finally he decided to let her sleep on. He had his evening meal and washed up with the rain water collected in an old earthen jar.

After washing up he had his usual evening smoke. He usually slept early but that night he did not. He laid a couple of old blankets on the earthen floor for himself and added more wood to the fire. Normally he would just let the fire die, but he thought she might feel cold in the middle of the night. Opening the back door he peed into the gutter. The few drops of urine spattering onto his feet were hot compared to the rain beating against him. The icy blast made him shiver. Quickly he bolted the door. Twice in the night he woke up to check on her. She was still febrile and somewhere toward morning she was delirious again.

The next morning the rain had stopped. The chirping of birds woke him up. The sky was deep blue and the air was crisp though a bit nippy. Already the morning sun was spreading its welcome rays everywhere. He boiled some water and baked some potatoes by wrapping them in mud and putting them over the hot embers. His stock of flour biscuits was running low. If he had time he would make some that day. It was convenient to prepare and apart from rice, the flour biscuits were almost his staple diet. He always added a liberal amount of salt to his flour biscuits. The salt replenished whatever he lost from sweating, especially if he had a long journey to make.

He was pouring hot water into a cup of coffee beans when she woke up and asked, "Where am I?"

"Ah, you are awake. There was a storm. You collapsed at my front door and I brought you in. You were hurt and bleeding. Would you like some food?"

"Yes, I feel hungry and weak."

"Don't try to walk. I will get you some porridge I cooked last night," he told her.

She was ravenous at first but after half a bowl she lost her appetite. "I feel dizzy," she said and lay on the bed again. "My name is Ma-Li. We live at Kampong Kepong.

"Some nights ago some communists attacked us. They raped the women and killed the men, even little boys. They accused us of

95

giving information to the police. One of them attempted to rape me but in the process I stabbed him with my knife. He fell dead on top of me and after the communists had gone I wandered off into the night.

"As I was leaving the village a storm came. I fell many times in the dark but kept on walking. It was awful. Everything was dark. I must have walked for miles. I saw a light far off and headed for it. I ended up at your place. You saved my life. I must thank you," Ma-Li said.

Somehow he did not believe her story. There were too many loose ends that did not tie up. She did not look as if she had been in the wilderness caught up in a storm for such a long time. Her attire, including the waterproof slicker, suggested that she was dressed for travelling. The wound on her thigh looked very fresh. If she had been bleeding for such a long time, she would have been dead.

But that was her business. In a couple of days when fully rested she would probably move off or go back to whatever place she came from.

"I have not done much for you. Only given you shelter," he replied.

"Oh, you saved my life. You stopped the bleeding. I would have been dead otherwise," she told him.

He felt the warmth rising to his cheeks and said, "I'm sorry. I hope you do not take offence. You were bleeding. When I was a little boy, I used to follow my grandfather around. He was a *sinseh*. I think the dressing needs to be changed. I shall gather some herbs and make you a poultice to treat the infection," he told her.

"It's very kind of you. I shall repay your kindness," she said.

He packed a few of the day's necessities in a sling and went off for the morning's expedition. The flood water had receded and the fields were green again. After walking a couple of miles he came upon a pond teeming with fish. He had a good catch of fish as well as four waterfowl and set out for the return journey. He collected some herbs for a poultice and was quite pleased with the morning's work.

When he returned, he noticed that she had cleaned herself, maybe even taken a bath. She looked like a changed woman and was certainly pretty. In fact, he had never seen a lovelier woman. She had also tidied up the hut. The woman's touch was evident. He saw some wet clothes on the lines, hers as well as his.

"I hope you do not mind my borrowing your shirt and pants. I had to wash mine," she said.

"You are most welcome, Ma-Li, to whatever is in the house. Look what I've got for us this morning." He showed her the morning's catch, proud of his day's achievements. He had his wash and set to prepare a poultice for her. When it was ready he passed it to her.

The days turned into nights and the nights into days. He had thought each morning that she would be moving along but she gave no inclination of leaving. He had not planned on that. In her own way she was helpful to him. She had taken over the housework and he had more time to work in the fields.

One afternoon when he came in for the mid-day meal he found her pale and clutching her abdomen.

"Are you sick, Ma-Li?" he enquired.

"I'll be all right. I have a little pain in my lower abdomen," she told him.

"Have you eaten anything unusual? Do you have diarrhoea?" he asked her.

"No diarrhoea, but there was some bleeding from the womb."

"Are you vomiting?" he asked her.

She nodded. "I think I'm having a baby."

"You have to rest. You should not do any more work. Would you like me to take you to a doctor? Or to some friends and relatives who could look after you?" he asked her, half hoping that she would say no.

"I've got nobody. No friends. I shall be all right. I will not give you trouble. I will work for you in return for shelter," she replied.

"Well, suit yourself, but don't exert yourself and do any work just yet," he added.

Ma-Li did as she was advised and at the end of the week was feeling fine.

They were living in a very secluded part of the country. The nearest neighbour was about three miles away. He was a farmer with a half a dozen children. When Ma-Li's time came he would ask the neighbour's wife to lend her a hand. The way the baby was growing, it looked as if it wouldn't be far off. Tomorrow, he thought to himself, he would pay a visit to the neighbour and maybe seek her advice and get some baby clothing.

When he told Mrs Chen about Ma-Li she too had her doubts

but they were centred on what he told her rather than the facts of Ma-Li's story as narrated by him. After all, he was a lonely bachelor and Ma-Li had been living with him for about eight months. It was more likely that he himself was the father of the unborn child.

When he left, Mr and Mrs Chen discussed the possibility, but they were happy for him. He had been living too much alone by himself and at one stage they even thought of matching him with one of Mrs Chen's cousins in the village.

It was evening by the time he got home. He was carrying a good load of old clothes and nappies as well as odds and ends including an old feeding bottle. Mrs Chen had told him that the maternal instinct in Ma-Li would tell her what all those things were for.

As soon as she showed the earliest sign of pain he was to run to Mrs Chen for help. Mrs Chen had told him that the onset of labour in a first-born would usually be prolonged and there would be ample time for him to run to their house and back. Mrs Chen wondered why he had never acquired a bicycle.

As he neared the hut he noticed that the door was ajar. Usually by this time Ma-Li would have lighted the lamp. Maybe she was tired and had fallen asleep. She would be cheered by the things he had brought back from the neighbours, he told himself.

As soon as he entered the door he knew that something was amiss. The house was in a shambles. Chairs and the table were overturned, food scattered on the ground, clothing strewn on the floor. He realised that the back door was open.

Ma-Li was sprawled face-down in the mud. One glance told him that she was dead. Whoever it was had ripped her clothing off and thrown them over her naked body. There was blood all over and he could see cuts and welts on her back, arms, and legs. There was a big cut on her head. Someone had rubbed her long glossy black hair in the mud.

He was nauseated by the brutality. He knelt down on the earth and gently turned her over. She had been slashed on the shoulders, breasts, and torso. He observed that where she had tried to ward off the attack the cuts had been inflicted deep over both forearms; some fingers were left dangling.

"Ma-Li, Ma-Li," he called to her in the hope that she might still be alive. Miraculously her puffed up blood-shot eyes opened. He propped her up. Blood was oozing from her mouth.

"What happened, Ma-Li?" he asked.

"The villagers — they came — committed — adultery — the child — proof. When they came — to kill him — he sent — me away. I found — your hut. Sor-ry — Sor rry . . ."

He put her head down gently on the wet ground and closed her eyelids. After squatting there for a long time, he stood up and made his way into the hut to fetch Ma-Li's blanket.

"Now I know, now I know," he repeated to himself. He had been suspicious of Ma-Li's earlier account but had been too polite to question her about it. Casting his eyes around the countryside he finally decided to bury her in the shade of an Angsana tree about two hundred yards away from his hut.

He spent the greater part of two hours digging Ma-Li's grave. Halfway through, he had to fetch his oil lamp as it was getting dark. At dusk he buried her together with the baby clothing and the old feeding bottle.

Back in the hut he arranged the table and a couple of chairs and sitting down he stared into the dark night. He heard the howl of the night wind and soon after felt its icy blast. He had forgotten to shut the door. Suddenly the pent-up emotions within him broke like a storm and burying his face in his hands he cried out "Ma-Li! Ma-Li!" and wept unashamedly.

Rite of Passage

Ho Poh Fun

She felt like a chattel, sitting next to Joachim in his car. His car, not hers. "We keep separate bank accounts too," she had told her friends. "There is nothing in this world like a truly independent woman."

Joachim had taken leave to be alone with her for a quiet holiday. She had proposed the idea in the soft and emotionless voice she had often used with the clients in her managerial office. Nearly three months ago. He had been busy attending to the details of protocol relating to some state matter and couldn't get away. She had reminded him again. It was to be in Singapore. A quiet holiday for two. She needed it, she had said.

For some time she had not been herself. She was consciously aware of it. She was undergoing some transformation, not only physically but also mentally. One moment she was raging steam. Another moment she felt cold and weighed down as if by a block of lead. She took leave from work. After two days, even the atmosphere of the home seemed repressive.

And now, sitting next to Joachim gave her the feeling of being transported—as if she were a box of goods to be delivered for storage in some prestigious firm. She seemed to have seen them before—those single neatly sealed packages—sitting sedately next to the driver's seat in an air-conditioned van or station wagon—always with the tag, "Fragile: Handle with Care"—handwritten. Or was this a figment of her imagination?

She threw a glance at Joachim. He was driving with all the concentration and self-consciousness of one who had a prized possession whom he must impress. After all, how often had he the opportunity

101

of having her seated quietly beside him in his car? Throughout the period of courtship and their two years of marriage, he could actually count the number of times he had had her in his car with him. She was the sort who liked to be in control behind the wheel and also to be in the position to account for her own mobilisation.

She thought she could award him good marks for steering manoeuvres. He skilfully negotiated a sharp bend without letting the engine drag, and allowed the car to pick up speed toward a junction where a security guard post was situated. The guards made no attempt to stop the car as it sailed past, with Joachim sitting very confidently behind the wheel. The car turned into a road lined with chalets, and its speed slackened considerably as it approached a narrow gravel path that wound a short distance up a slope. It finally stopped in front of a chalet marked "A." It was a chalet for administrative officers who held important positions in the civil service. Constructed originally for British colonial staff on holiday, the chalet and others of similar design had been made available to local administrative officers ever since Singapore attained independent status. With maternal and paternal relatives solidly established within statutory boards and the civil service, she had been in and out of holiday bungalows ever since she was a child. This one looked smaller than some in which she had lodged, but it was certainly no less elegantly styled than her parents' house at Upper East Coast Road, and she was sure it would prove no less comfortable than their recently renovated home at Swiss Club Road.

She did not wait to be helped out. As a child she used to spring out at her own peril even before the engine had been switched off. But now, even as the impulse arose, her movements were slow. As she stepped gingerly onto the grass, Joachim slammed his side of the car door and rushed to her aid. She wasn't exactly sure whether she ought to feel grateful. She had always disapproved of public display of affection. As if the woman couldn't hold her own in open spaces. But today her feet felt wobbly.

As she turned toward the house, he started searching in his pockets for the keys. During the journey to the chalet, he had told her how he had called personally to check on the exact location of the chalet that had been allotted to him. Tongue in cheek he had told her how he had instructed the caretaker to send someone to do some scrupulous cleaning. Just in case. There weren't to be any of those slimy or crawly things around. No spiders. No cockroaches. No lizards. No snails. His wife was very particular about where she put her head each night, he had said.

He would now like to see her properly resting after the long drive. They were at the porch, and she stood awkwardly, though now more steadily, having exercised her legs. She looked at Joachim, his face flushed with an air of expectation. There was always a child-like quality about him that she found irresistible. Yet people who knew him at work had thought him stern, authoritative, even un-approachable. She turned to gaze down the grassy slope at the white-walled chalets standing erect and still at intervals apart. All of them looked unoccupied as she could not detect any clothesline or parked car. There were sprigs of sunshine on the ground within the shade of trees, and these transposed into varying shapes as the wind blew.

How long ago was it since she stopped holidaying in bungalows or chalets such as these? Probably since the fateful event. But four or five times a year, in the fifties and the sixties, one relative or another would extend invitations for a change of air. There were beaches around Katong, Siglap, and Bedok—but Changi could provide facilities not found elsewhere.

That was before it became fashionable to holiday abroad. Amahs would be given leave or instructed to spring clean their employers' houses whilst whole families gathered at some holiday bungalow or chalet, and tolerated each person's presence for one or two days under cramped living conditions, presided over by the reigning matriarch—her mother's mother—about whom she felt a certain dread. The lady hailed from Malacca and had a high forehead and neat upswept hair, still miraculously black and formidably gold-hairpinned in the traditional way. She had found it difficult to accept, let alone understand, how one woman—unschooled, thoroughly domesticated, and widowed—could yet command the attention of two generations. At her approach, even the most disdainful of men turned meek, while the women hastened to court favours. A kind of communal intimacy was cultivated where individual concerns became common property. There they sat, probing thickly into the affairs of so-and-so, arbitration withheld until after the matriarch had made an appearance.

Joachim had by now unlocked the front door of the chalet and returned to the car to unload the provisions. She entered the house on her own, noting by the thin air of disinfectant that the place had been recently cleaned. Directly in front of her as she entered the foyer, a long staircase rose tongue-like to the right. She crossed the foyer with its potted green plants to inspect the rest of the ground floor. She didn't open locked doors. She was satisfied with the state of the kitchen and the adjoining storeroom. She was pleased with the spaciously designed and simply, but tastefully furnished, dining hall and sitting room. She returned to the porch. Joachim was still bending over some boxes in the boot. He looked up when she appeared, and grinned. "I'll fix you a beef steak for dinner," he said. She didn't feel like having a beef steak. But it would not do to say no. She felt like moving forward to help, but drew back, remembering her condition.

She was more than six months big with child and nearly forgot that she had now to constantly hold back her shoulders to maintain a balanced pose. She was carrying his child, and it was good to see him so thoughtful and considerate. After he had carried all the boxes to the kitchen, he helped her upstairs, insisting that she lie down to rest in one of the rooms. She assured him that she felt fine. He nodded silently and returned to sort out the provisions and to store what needed to be stored in the storeroom.

She found the plan of the upstairs floor exactly what she had imagined it to be—which was remarkable but not strange, considering that all the chalets situated on that side of the road were of similar design, and she being no stranger to these chalets. She noticed that Joachim had not brought up their personal things. She poked her head out at the top of the stairs and called to him. He responded with alacrity.

She headed for the master bedroom, pushing two canvas bags mounted on wheels, one of which, containing her belongings, was rather shiny and new, shaped like a long sack. Crossing the room, she threw open the windows of opaque glass, and looked out at one of them taking in the placid view of the white and grey painted walls of the differently styled chalets across the road with their gleaming doors and mysterious windows peeping behind the foliage of straggly trees. It would be good to go for a stroll after dinner, she thought. Then as if some automatonic machine button had been pressed, she uttered aloud, "We shall set out at dawn to watch the sun shatter the darkness."

Strange that the words of a bygone past should come to mind. They rang like incantation to her ears. Jo Jo had initiated this string of words one night, perhaps in this very room itself, so many years ago. Strange too that she should bring Jo Jo to mind again. It could have happened just yesterday. Some Ceylonese and Eurasian friends from nearby chalets were going to hold a beach party. Jo Jo wanted to attend. Consent was not given. Jo Jo had turned sixteen and thought she was old enough to take care of herself. In a storm of tears, Jo Jo ran upstairs, entered the room where she and Marcella were playing "Snap," slammed the door, and started voicing her frustration and anger. Then, with a gleam in her eyes, Jo Jo said that she would act in defiance of the adults. She would sneak out at dawn to watch the sun rise in the east. On hearing this, Marcella simply gaped. She alone offered to accompany Jo Jo. Turning to her with a wide smile, and narrowing her eyes, Jo Jo mysteriously said, "We shall set out at dawn to watch the sun shatter the darkness."

She was two years younger than Jo Jo. Jo Jo always knew best. Marcella studied at St. Hilda's, Joan and Elsie studied at Katong Convent, whilst she, Clara, and Edith studied at Kuo Chuan Girls'. Only Jo Jo studied in town. Each time they met at the usual gathering of relatives, there was a harvest of information available. Jo Jo would fill the girls up on events and sights around town. "Town" consisted of the city area around Bras Basah Road, Dhoby Ghaut, Orchard Road, and North Bridge Road. Jo Jo had a dozen friends in those places and often went gallivanting around the Pavilion, Cathay Cinema, Rex Book Store, Magnolia Snack Bar, and Odeon Cinema. There were dragons and tigresses embedded in the many characters she described and the various skirmishes with danger, but the most absorbing was still Jo Jo's account of scaling the ninety-nine steps of the steep slope behind the Cathay Cinema. Sneaking off with Jo Jo to the beach to watch the sun rise was an experience not to be missed.

It was dark when they sneaked out of the room which housed all the girl cousins. They were in their lawn nightdresses—Jo Jo confident and sure as she led the way, she slightly apprehensive now at the thought of penetrating the streaming darkness. The experience was like a baptism. The air was dank. The grass was wet although it had not rained. The hems of their dresses were soaked by the time their feet touched sand. The sky, she remembered, was an unimpressive grey. The moon was still high—glimmerings of its presence hanging wet and suspended on trees. As from the fangs of a dragon, an irregular spread of fiery light had already burst forth, extending beyond a part of the sky that merged with the sea. She looked at Jo Jo who kept mouthing the words, "Watch the sun shatter the darkness . . . Watch the sun shatter the darkness . . ." The words embodied a rhythm that was hypnotising. She wished Jo Jo would stop. She struggled against being carried away by the tide that was beginning to sound like a supernatural chant. But Jo Jo stood enthralled as the light climbed higher and higher, her eyes wide and open to the source of disseminating warmth. She tugged at Jo Jo's sleeve. It was time to return before their absences were discovered.

She stood rigid and still by the area of the windows as if entranced by a vision of the past. A breeze blew in and fanned her brow. She became conscious of a heat building up inside her. She walked to another window that looked seaward. Beyond the tiled rooftops and wavering green of foliage, the sea spread wide and open to the sky. As she gazed hard and long at the liquid expanse, a part of her seemed to be dissolving. When she turned back into the room, surely a part of her had dissipated. She tried, but her eyes could not focus well enough to make out the sharp contours of the objects in the room. Her senses swimming, she grasped a window latch, leaned back, and lapsed into a yoga-like stillness. By the time she opened her eyes, her vision had cleared. She moved languidly to where she had dumped the bags. The sight of them brought her back to where she had left off.

She had been determined to bring only the essentials on this occasion, but already they looked like a lot. Her belongings filled the canvas bag which measured high and rectangular to her waist and also spilled into the canvas bag that was supposed to carry only Joachim's things. Joachim had laughed at her at their hotel suite at the Miramar in Hong Kong when he saw her unpack. He had just emerged from the bathroom and turned amusement to laughter at the sight of her surrounded by cosmetics, toiletries, towels, thermal underwear, and piles of dresses. Legs still dripping wet under the bathrobe, he had said teasingly: "One would have thought you had moved house!" Impulsively she threw him a towel.

She was holding a towel now and didn't know what to do with it. She quickly put it down. She thought of him as she unwrapped their day clothes, slipped hangers into them, and hung them up in the closet. Then she unrolled some brown paper she had brought along to line the bare shelves. After cutting some sheets down to size, she fitted them neatly over the wooden boards before pushing in the night clothes, towels, and undergarments. Just as she was attempting to slide back the doors of the closet, one of the panels slipped. It was on the verge of falling out and she avoided being hit just in time by throwing her entire bodily weight against it. Having gained control of the situation, she slowly brought the panel down and laid it against the wall.

She walked over to the bed and sat down. The incident had certainly sharpened her responses, but it was quite a while before her breathing returned to normal. She wondered whether she had damaged any internal tissue or had in any way affected the foetus. She looked at the closet where Joachim's and her things had been placed. There was something jarring about a closet half-closed. She dived a hand into her canvas bag and started drawing out its contents. There now spread before her the paraphernalia she could hardly do without: cleansers, lipstick, moisturisers, hairbrush, comb, first-aid plaster, cotton wool, safety pins, toothbrush, toothpaste, tranquillizers, cologne, flannel cloths, talcum powder, tissue paper, hand mirror, powder compact, torchlight, her favourite Kawabata novel, a notebook containing all the relevant telephone numbers . . . She felt quite tired just at looking at the clutter. Carrying these to the dressing table, she found space for some of them in drawers, and arranged the rest on the surface boards. Relieved, she sank onto the cushioned stool before the mirror.

She unpinned her hair and gave it a few quick strokes with her hairbrush prior to running a comb swiftly and smoothly through it. She and Jo Jo had been fascinated by hair. They had probably sunk a sizeable fortune into it, nourishing and conditioning it, experimenting with various brands of hair shampoo, creme rinses, hair tonic, beauty packs, styling lotion, and hair spray. Jo Jo's hair was beautifully dark and straight. Hers was wavy. Was it a myth that straight hair grew faster than wavy? Jo Jo had said that straight hair would. They had competed to see whose front line hair could be combed over to touch the tip of the chin first. Hers did. It was probably because she had a lower forehead. She didn't really want to win after winning, and tried to pacify the indignant Jo Jo who had never before had to bow out the loser in any challenge. The "angri-fied" Jo Jo had her hair trimmed very short. Almost like Twiggy's. A few weeks later, she too sported short hair. Something had happened. Family and relatives now regarded her as the new Jo Jo. Rather it was Jo Jo's non-conformity. Jo Jo's pride. Jo Jo's drive. She wore short hair for a few years. Then she met Joachim. Joachim said he was crazy about girls with long hair. He simply worshipped her in a chignon.

She gazed at herself in the mirror and wondered whether she could ever be assigned a fixed personality. She emulated Jo Jo. Now she wanted to please Joachim. She once heard it said that women belie their own existence. The speaker, she recalled, was the wife of a foreign diplomat. The madame had read philosophy in a French university prior to coming to Singapore. What is woman but scepticism and veiling dissimulation? It was so much easier to be a man—physically, mentally, and socially.

Which was the real she? Surely the one she had been familiar with for the past five years. Prior to that she had been job-hopping, never quite certain what she wanted. She spent her time taking up language and business courses, and even took time to do sustained service at the Home for the Retarded. She had worked briefly as an administrative assistant in a government department, then as secre-tary to the manager of a shipping company, then a desk job at a hotel in Tanglin Road before meeting her present employer who, for reasons of his own, offered her a post in his large trading firm. The post was not prestigious but the work was challenging. Surely she had proven an ability to hold her own on important matters. Within five years of joining the trading company, she had risen to the rank of general manager. She had cultivated links with major import and export firms in all the ASEAN states. She had entertained trade missions from Hong Kong, Taiwan, Korea, Sri Lanka, and Bulgaria. She had indeed personally contributed to the expansion of the company which had recently opened a second warehouse in Jurong.

She had met Joachim about three years ago at a luncheon party organised by her employer for his close business associates and senior staff. Joachim was the nephew of one of her employer's personal friends. He was then an administrative officer attached to the Ministry of Labour. Just before their marriage, he had been trans-ferred to the Finance Ministry. If anyone were to ask her about her marriage to Joachim, she would probably say, "I was engulfed. I succumbed."

She had kept Jo Jo at the back of her mind all these years. Yet Jo Jo had been the prime influence in her formative years. Now the spectre of Jo Jo loomed large. Jo Jo was probably the first person she knew who could dance the twist, then the rage in the early sixties—"Just imagine you are holding the end of a bath towel in each hand, Annie, and trying to rub your back dry after a shower. The rhythm will come . . ." Jo Jo was also probably the first Chinese girl she knew who dared to wear a bikini, to the chagrin of her parents. "I am not wearing a bikini to attract any boy," Jo Jo had said. "I wear it to please myself." Jo Jo looked very haughty when she spoke. Jo Jo had a long slim body and small undeveloped breasts. She stalked away with such straight-limbed grace.

She was lean, like Jo Jo. But Joachim had thought her very well proportioned, contrary to what she had read about men's passion for women. "You are quite unlike all the other girls I have met. Bulges all over the place," he had said. He had seen her mother and was convinced that she wouldn't grow into a shapeless mass by the time she reached middle age. She had needed reassurance. He gave it.

She now sat with her head cocked, luxuriating in the feel of the air piling and spreading restfully around her. Somewhere a lone bird twittered and out at sea the throbbing of a motor launch could be discerned. There was no Jo Jo. Yet she could almost feel Jo Jo's very presence in the room: Jo Jo's quick excited laughter as she tilted her head in response to a joke . . . Jo Jo solemn and cutting as she spoke out about some adult issue . . . Jo Jo's mimicry of the voices and gestures of some adult members of the extended family . . . Jo Jo helping her to fit into a new swimsuit, both of them giggling behind closed doors . . . Jo Jo in dungarees, her clear chiming voice leading a group of younger children in "Simon Says" . . . Jo Jo humming "Plaisir d'Amour" and looking deceptively romantic as she drifted down the stairs in a haze of chiffon . . .

What would Jo Jo have to say about what ranged before her now? Surely she could remember as she remembered—the clutter of game-sets, stuffed toys, and comic books strewn untidily in rooms, the porches heavy with tobacco smoke as the men gathered there to discuss the mayor's next move at City Hall, or the latest entries in the official gazette, the women's voices vibrating amidst the bustle in the kitchen as they pounded chilli and *blachan*, peeled onions, skinned prawns, cleaned fish, or picked bean sprouts. Surely Jo Jo too could recall the afternoon spreads of *popia*, *laksa*, or *mee siam* dishes prepared by the collective body of women who seemed to prefer a lived life in the kitchen. And the late afternoons and evenings made palatable and intoxicating by the fragrance of *pulut* cooked with *pandan* leaves—and the rich brew of coffee which the men mixed with spirits.

And could she not also remember the women walking leisurely to the water's edge in makeshift swimming garments—sarongs tightly wrapped or knotted over their breasts—infants in hand or in arms? She could hear the infants shrieking, gurgling, or chortling, clutching their colourful plastic or rubber buoys upon contact with water, and the women smiling in a hesitant, faltering way—as if conscious only of the infants in tow and of the edges of their sarongs getting increasingly soaked and seeming to fall out of place with every turn of wave.

Jo Jo would say, "I disapprove of them—these women—their faces smelling of *bedak sejok* or the latest Merle Norman or Max Factor make-up. At each gathering you'd see them—our mothers too— in their latest collection of jewellery—their arms bejewelled or gold-bangled—a modest *intan* at least on one finger. And they always assume a naïvete don't they, in the company of patronising males? Feminine virtue, my foot! Sheer apathy, I call it. And they exhibit no end of greed where food is concerned. I just saw two of them gorging themselves with food with the appetite of sows in a slough. Very foxy too—why, just the other day, I overheard one of them relating to a group of them at the kitchen how cleverly she had succeeded in getting the grocer to supply more than she actually paid. How did the rest react to the tale? You wouldn't believe this—they actually applauded. I ran away as fast as I could from the scene, with the sounds of them cackling like witches in my ears. Had to, you know. Pretty contagious!"

She put her comb down and looked fixedly into the mirror. The face of Jo Jo looked out at her. "Hello, Annie," it said. Now a wide-eyed gamine stared back. It wasn't Jo Jo that she saw. How could she? She blinked. There was no mistaking. A gamine with the clear gleaming eyes of Jo Jo beamed back. The gamine turned, her slenderness displayed in a dress that Jo Jo used to wear. The gamine threw her head back—a cascade of fine wavy hair tumbled down her neck and shoulders. But it was her hair, not Jo Jo's. Jo Jo had cut hers, remember? The day she cut it, she had hired a motor launch and headed off to sea to meet some boys who were canoeing off Pulau Tekong. Now a tablet of stone bearing the name, Josephine Tan Bee Neo, marked the site of an empty grave.

She grasped the strands of hair together, ran a comb swiftly through it, and knotted it into a pony tail. I am Annie, not Jo Jo, she told the image in the mirror. But didn't Jo Jo have long hair too, once? Jo Jo. Always Jo Jo. I am Annie, ANNIE! Pressing a few loose strands back from her face, she rose from her seat.

You were swimming out at sea when your foot touched the fin of some misbegotten sea monster. The creature with its headful of hair, thin shoulders, and heavy inertness swam before her in the mirror. A tight scream pierced the air. Did it come from her? Hands clenched, she closed her eyes and felt the darkness weighing down on her as she groped for the bed. Sinking into the soft springs, she could feel her heart palpitating violently, as the weight of the unborn bore hard and heavy into her bones. "Women never are the same again once they've been trapped with a lead weight in their bodies," Jo Jo had said. Folding her arms resolutely in front of her, she hugged herself and tried to fight back the tears.

A hand gripped her shoulder. She looked up. Joachim's face peered down. She thrust aside all efforts to hold her and backed away as if terrified. He waited. He was at a loss as to what he should do. It seemed to him that her present condition could yield no place for him. Finally she let her arms drop. Turning her face toward his, she spoke in a low drowned voice: "I hate myself for this."

He went to her, wound his arms around her swollen form, and sank his face into the folds of her dress. She did not appear to feel his presence as she gazed past him, over his head and across the room to the light streaming in at the door. A girl, slim and flat bellied, her hair flying, had just leapt through it, her slippers flapping furiously and unceremoniously down the long staircase, and out along the gravel path till they were muffled and silenced forever in the accommodating beach sand and roar of the insouciant ocean. She leaned forward to speak, her eyes wet and staring. A wave of emotion overtook her original intent. Shaking uncontrollably, she stretched out her hands to grip the edge of the bed. Her fingers kept slipping

111

and slipping. Overwhelmed, she sank back—her legs parting. Then the tears welled forth even more, flooding her cheeks and blurring her vision of the surroundings.

A Dream of China

Ovidia Yu

He was a drab old man in worn clothes and he spoke with the querulousness of one who has long known that Fate holds a grudge against him. He wanted to come back to Singapore. I thought of my modern little flat and my husband and babies and I couldn't imagine the man sleeping on our Italian-leather sofa. I want to see your father again, the drab old man unwisely said. That sealed the matter. I did not want him to see my father again. If I had anything to do with it, he would never see my father again. The sad, sly eyes lost the watery hold they had gained on my sympathy. My mind, which had been wondering where an extra bed could be fitted, dropped the matter and began to cast about for a diplomatic way to say "No."

My father is a good man. My mother—his second wife—died soon after I was born and my father retired in order to devote his time to bringing me up. Until then, he had been a marine biologist at the University of Singapore. He still turned out an occasional article on sea worms in between teaching me the right way to hold a Chinese calligraphy brush or telling me stories. As I grew up and he grew older, his stories dwelt with increasing frequency on China.

China was the most beautiful of beautiful lands. In his youth he had wandered within her bosom and penetrated the depths of her heart. He had seen strange monkeys with white faces and snakes in the bellies of other snakes. He had shot white water rapids, climbed hundreds of steps to stone temples, and trekked her forests.

"When we went to America to visit your Second Sister," he would say to me, "the forests there reminded me so much of China. The Catskill Mountains especially reminded me of home."

After 50 years in Singapore, "home" for him was still Szechuan.

My elder sisters and brother, all children of his first marriage and many years older than I, warned me. "Whenever he sees anything particularly beautiful he says that's how it is in China. You mustn't believe all of it, you know!"

They were sorry for me, a child living in the company of an old man who told the same stories over and over again. But children love repetition and I thrived on it. I began to dream dreams of China on this island Singapore. The strange mountains and still waters. The weird beast (was it a unicorn? I was certain it was a unicorn, the strangest and most magical of all beasts) that appeared only when some momentous event was about to break on the land. In China there were fat laughing fairies that could adopt fantastic shapes. There were spirits in the trees and animals. All this was much more interesting than the Western fairy stories with their brashly coloured illustrations of Caucasians with wings. More interesting, too, than mundane life in Singapore, where the closest thing to magic was the haunted cubicle in the primary school toilet. (A severed foot was frequently to be seen there. If you pressed it you could see bones through the skin.)

But one thing about China lay heavy on my father's conscience. Because of that, he had decided that he would die in exile, never to return.

After the Second World War, when the Japanese surrendered Singapore and left China, my father and his younger brother faced a choice. They could stay in Singapore or they could return to build a new China. In their youth—and they were still young then—the brothers had been revolutionaries. Both had defied their father in leaving home to join the army fighting to bring a new lease on life to the corrupt and dying nation they loved. As teenagers they had seen China through the eyes of the privileged, as sons of the wealthy. In the army and disowned by their father, they saw her differently. Bruised and savaged but nonetheless beautiful. Perhaps even more so, because now her pulse beat in their bodies and their blood soaked her rich but parched soil. It is hard to understand the allure of a beautiful and troubled land, but it was in China then.

At that time, my father had a steady income from teaching, in Singapore. He had his wife and my eldest sister, who was already born. He elected to stay in Singapore. It was this decision that in later years he regarded as his supreme act of cowardice. His younger brother returned to China to help repair the atrocities of the Japanese. He remained in Singapore.

My father pined for China, seeing his act of selfishness reflected in the shallowness of the lives his students at the university led. All they did was study. If they did dream, it was of job security and owning a car. Most of his students were Chinese but they did not have the backbone and determination he thought characterised Chinese youth. That which his younger brother had and he lacked!

My eldest sisters and brother laughed at him. The youth of Singapore are practical, my third sister would say. Do you want them to go around with slogans and Molotov cocktails when they don't see anything wrong with the country? And my brother would ask, what do you think is wrong with Singapore? My father could see only one thing wrong with Singapore, but that one thing summed up everything else: Singapore was not China.

He had failed to return to China as his brother had. His younger brother had done right and he had done wrong. He was too overcome by shame to return himself later, when he was no longer needed.

"But lots of people go 'round China on the tours," my brother tried to persuade him. "They have special tours just for old people, you know. You're always talking about going back. Why don't you go now? You may not have many years left, you know. I'll pay for the trip, of course. I'll set up everything, in fact. I already checked it up. There's a tour group leaving in the second week of June. Why don't you let me get you a place on that one, Pa?"

My brother is well-meaning and not easy to dissuade, but my father dissuaded him. My father felt he did not deserve to see China again, much as he longed to. Instead he wrote poems in Chinese about living in exile, and in Singapore tried to live as he felt a true Chinese would.

He was Westernised to a certain extent and did not demand unquestioning obedience from his children. It was not in that that he remained staunchly Chinese, but in his calm, his respect for the "face" of the servants, and his disregard for material gain.

"The Chinese aren't really like that at all!" my second sister told me. My second sister who married an American Jew. "The Chinese are as bad as the Jews when it comes to making money!" She talked as though she weren't Chinese herself, often speaking of "We

115

Americans," but her American accent could not alter her almond eyes and high cheekbones.

My father sympathised with her son, Golden Dragon, who smoked opium and wore a Jewish skull cap atop his Chinese-style plait. He was trying to unearth his roots, his identity as a human being. "Without the human experience of your forefathers before you it is hard to build a strong future," my father said. We knew he was thinking not only of his Eurasian grandson but of his children who had never seen the graves of the ancestors in Szechuan.

The years passed. I discovered that not everyone viewed China as my father did. The Red Guards took over all of China and overseas Chinese sent money, woollen clothes, and pity to those left behind. Even this twisted the thorn in my father's side as he lived in ease away from his country instead of suffering with her.

I learnt more about my father's feelings after I married. He confided in my husband things that he could not tell me, a girl child. My husband, however, had no such scruples and passed them on to me.

It was not only shame for ignoring the call of his country that had barred my father from China all these years, Heavenly Wisdom said. There was also the letter which his brother had written to him when he had reconsidered and spoken of returning to China only months after his brother. (Heavenly Wisdom guessed that my father's younger brother had taken over the household of their late father and what was left of the wealth of their family. If my father returned, all would have to be surrendered to him, who was the eldest son of the family.) The letter said my father should not return if he had any regard for their family. He who had married without their parents' consent, whose wife was used to city life in Singapore. Would his wife pine to return to Singapore, causing their lands to be disrupted and sold to support her in luxury? My father could not say no with certainty. He felt shame that his younger brother was wiser than he in such matters. He thought his younger brother would serve family interests far better than he could, and resolved not to displace such a dutiful son by returning himself. Since then, he had looked upon his younger brother as a paragon of virtue and dutiful good sense.

"I didn't know he ever meant to go back to China," I said to my husband, surprised. "He never told me that."

"That was in 1946, I think," Heavenly Wisdom said absently. "Long before your time. Anyway, after the Red Guards took it all over there was no question of going back."

"And he didn't go back after he decided to just because of a letter his brother wrote him? That doesn't sound like Pa. Are you sure? I would have gone back anyway, and claimed everything that was mine by right!"

"There's no point discussing the past. Living in China during the Cultural Revolution would have been no joke. It's a good thing your father didn't go back."

"But he could have gone back to China and taken everything and come back to Singapore and then he would be rich as well as free," I argued.

My husband shook his head mildly. "If he had gone back to China he would never have left again. Baby One is eating my black socks."

Heavenly Wisdom always referred to our sons as Baby One and Baby Two. When they ate socks and mosquito coil, he regarded their diet with detached scientific interest. For that reason, in the early years of our marriage, I had little time to think further on the subject of my father and his younger brother in China.

Some old people become invalids because they feel without a place in society. The role of invalid is easy to assume and is self-sustaining. My father did not allow me to make him an invalid. After I married, he moved to Pasir Ris where he spent his days planting orchids, writing poems about exile, and drinking tiger bone wine. He had never given up his interest in calligraphy. Often my husband and I took the babies on the long drive up to Pasir Ris, where their grandfather taught their infant hands to hold the Chinese brush in the correct way and told them stories about China. At low tide my father and my husband walked on the seabed barefoot. They had a scientific game which involved spotting sea worms and giving their scientific names. As these were serious scientific expeditions, the babies and I were never allowed to go with them but had to stay in the house.

It was during one of their scientific expeditions that I came across some of my father's poems while cleaning his study room. The babies were asleep under the fan and my father never minded me reading his poetry. I found my favourite one that went:

Lovely silent carp
Circling my ornamental pond
Like a wise thought.
Is all water your element
Or do you dream of wide brimming rivers
As I have a dream of home?

Surely my father was content in Singapore after all these years? But it was still an ornamental pond and not the wide brimming river. Not home. My father's writing made me homesick for the China I had never known. Now, that was beautiful poetry. It stirred up feelings inside as well as pleased the ear and the eye.

At the back of the book of manuscripts there was a packet of letters I had not seen before. I could not resist letters from China, so I sat and read them. They were all from the wife of my father's younger brother and they were all letters asking for money to be sent.

"Did you send money?" I asked my father when he and my husband returned. He was not surprised that I had been reading his old letters.

"Yes, I believe I did," he said matter-of-factly. He took the letters from me and looked at them, vaguely perplexed.

"More money than he should have. It's a good thing I am not the sort of man to marry for dowry!" my husband said, in a buoyant mood. I could tell he had won their scientific game that day.

"I would not have given my daughter away to such a sort of man!" my father replied, pretending great dignity.

"But why were they always asking for money if, after all, my uncle returned to build a new China? Don't they treat him well there then? And why does my uncle's wife write instead of him writing you yourself? I could not write to Heavenly Wisdom's family for money."

One of my babies began to cry for me. Heavenly Wisdom went off to see to it and through the doorway I saw him trying to establish if babies ate seaweed. My babies did not and they both began to cry with great vigour. For that reason, my father's reply escaped me.

"Your uncle may have taken a mistress, neglecting his wife," Heavenly Wisdom suggested that night. "His wife might be too ashamed to let her family know and so is forced to write to your father for assistance."

But that was just speculation on Heavenly Wisdom's part. My father was not disposed to discuss the issue again, and I was left to wonder.

Then I was offered a chance to go to China. It was a university literary tour. Young people in Singapore don't speak Chinese as the older generation did. These young Singaporeans could read and write beautifully literate Chinese but were awkward when it came to conversation. I was invited to go on the tour as an interpreter, and because it was thought I knew something about China, being my father's daughter. The professor who organised the trip was a friend of my husband's. He made me the offer through my husband. Half of my expenses would be paid for. It was my opportunity, at last, to see the land of my people.

I wanted to go on the tour very badly, but it was not in my place to say so and I waited, trying to look patient, as my husband made up his mind.

My husband did not have much enthusiasm for China. His parents had never spoken to him of China except of their relief to have left in time. To him, China had been a land of corruption and oppression where whole families starved to death and daughters were sold. The new China, waving the banner of communism, hardly appealed to him more. All he liked about China was summed up in his liking Chinese acrobats. I did not expect him to sanction my leaving him and the babies for such a trip.

"You may go if you wish," my husband said.

"You will have to pay for half the trip, they only pay half," I reminded him.

"Do you doubt I can do that?" Heavenly Wisdom asked drily. So it was settled and I went to China for two weeks.

It is not my intention to describe China. I am writing of my family . . . my father and his younger brother.

A mission I had set for myself in China was to visit my father's hometown where my uncle and his wife still lived. There were few other relatives left alive. The tour brought us within two hours of my destination. Apparently, two hours' travel is an immense distance to most people in China, where they often calculate distance by bicycle rather than by car. However, I was able to rent a car, and two students and a guide set off with me. As we travelled through farmland and small city regions where bamboo scaffolding obscured most of the small buildings, I could not imagine my father there.

True, there was much beauty in China. On a boat trip the day before, we had all been stunned by the breathtaking loveliness of the river, nearby mountains with caves of stalactites, and distant mountains dreamy and purple in their vagueness. This was a China even my father had been unable to convey to me. It seemed a journey not just down river but back through time into an age of timelessness.

But seeing the Chinese people I felt glad I was a tourist. China spoke to my mind. The idea that this land was the land my people had sprung from, had lived off in pre-history, warmed and stirred me. However, China had nothing to say to my spirit, if indeed land speaks to spirit. My spirit was as alien here as I was. It inclined toward a diamond city of trees and meaningful occupation, efficiently sparkling in the modern world. That was where I truly belonged, among skyscrapers with glass fronts and gold-encrusted orchids. When I finally met my uncle, it was as a visitor to a strange land, not as a returning exile.

When I finally met my uncle I saw he had the face of my father. He was thin, shrivelled up. He spat noisily and conspicuously and, asked if he had any message for my father, said: "Tell him to send money."

I stayed to dine with my aunt and uncle, the students and guide dining at the foreigners-only hotel where we were to spend the night. I tried to remember everything I could. My father would treasure every detail I could give him. There was the small room we ate in, and another smaller one leading off that. There were black and white photographs and a few books. The food was simple and well prepared. All through the meal my uncle swore continuously at his wife and at my father. My father must have known it would come to this, he said. That was why he had not returned. He had always been the smart one. Why had my father not warned him? He had let him walk right into the jaws of it! If my father had only given him a word of warning he would now be in Singapore living in the lap of luxury, not being miserable and badly treated in this hovel, married to this misery of a wife that deserved to be dead.

I felt sorry for him. After all, he had the face of my father. I thought of my father serene in his garden, making scientific notes in his study room, and blessed the circumstances that had kept him from China.

120

Surely my father sent him money?, I asked, knowing that he did. Under my uncle's loud confusion of never asking my father for charity, never getting any money from my father, and never getting enough money from my father, my aunt softly said: "Yes, your father sends money. He is too good to us. Your uncle knows but will not admit it. Too proud."

I did not want to venture another remark. My aunt nervously pressed me to eat more, to the accompaniment of my uncle's muttered swearing and self-pity.

I gave my uncle the money my father had given me for him, and a tape recorder and camera. My uncle complained because my father had not thought to send cigarettes and because only one roll of film came with the camera. What good would the camera be to him after that? He could not afford more film himself, surely I could see that! But my aunt asked me to convey their thanks to my father. They might sell the camera, she said. It would keep them going well for some time. As my uncle stood under the lightbulb examining the camera and tape recorder and grumbling under his breath, my aunt and I washed the dinner bowls in a basin she brought to the table.

"He denounced some of my relatives," my aunt told me in a low voice. "Now my family won't have anything to do with us. Neither will his family. I don't blame them. He betrayed his own cousin on his mother's side. We are barely tolerated by people even now. The village children throw names at him and their parents encourage them. He will not work. He will not even ask for money. I have to do that." She sighed softly, and the hair straggling onto her face was yellow-white. "Your father always sends money when I ask for it, always a little more than I ask for. He is a good man."

"Yes," I agreed.

We talked softly about different family members and what they were doing. Soon my uncle aroused himself and announced that he was going to walk me to the hotel. I bowed goodbye to my aunt. Shaking hands seemed too forward and Western. She told me again to remember to give their thanks and regards to my family, especially my father.

The October night was chilly. There were many dark shapes out walking in brisk silence. My uncle and I added ourselves to the number. There were yellow puddles of street light with great pools of darkness in between. We walked from puddle to puddle in silence. Finally we reached the hotel.

"We leave again early tomorrow. We are to rejoin our group at lunch," I said awkwardly. "I suppose I shan't see you again this time."

This man who was my father's brother looked hungrily past me at the gate of the hotel compound.

"The only time we get to go inside is if a foreigner invites us in as guests," he said pointedly. "There is a canteen where you can buy me a drink. It has been years since I was invited to have a drink here."

"Why don't you come in for a drink?" I invited him lamely. He accepted with child-like excitement, panting a little in his eagerness as I held the compound gate open and the gate-keeper waved us both by without checking identification.

With great grandness, my uncle ordered orange drinks from the waiter. He criticised the glasses as dirty when the drinks arrived and insisted on new ones. To this man my father had trusted the honour of his family, now scattered and in disharmony. Could he live with that?, I wondered. One thing that had soothed his spirit in the long years of "exile" was the thought that he had done right in leaving everything to his brother who was a nobler person than he. I stared at the man gulping flat orange juice and felt a growing distaste. My father had made a mistake there! But this man had done me a great service by his greed. He had kept my father in Singapore. For that I owed him much.

I kept buying him the orange drinks he swallowed with such relish. I could not think of anything more I could do.

Finally, he let me walk him through the compound to the gate. Just inside the wall he turned and took one of my hands in both of his and he cried. Tears and yellow-streaked saliva dripped off his chin. I didn't know what to say, wishing with all my heart I had not come to China, not stirred up dormant feelings in this pathetic wreck of a man. When he calmed down, I patted him on the shoulder.

"We will send you things from Singapore," I promised. "My father will send things to you."

"Can you get me out of China?" he asked. "I want to come back to Singapore. Just me, one person. No wife."

Where would he live in Singapore? Not with my father. There

was little room in Pasir Ris. There was little room in our flat too. I couldn't have him sleep on the sofa! And what about his wife, alone in China?

"I want to see your father again," the man said. An angry, cheated look had come back into his eyes. He obviously felt that my father owed him much.

No. I would not do this to my father. I wanted to return to Singapore to tell him my uncle was well in China. That he was too busy (not too lazy) to write himself. My father could then breathe easy, believe he had done a good thing and reap in his old age his reward for the good life he had lived and the children he had reared. This man must not be allowed to come and spoil everything!

"Don't leave me to die here. I have not long to live. I want to get out. Can you get me out?"

"I will see to it when my father has left this world," I said. My father would not consider it a curse even if he knew and I would not tell him. "After that we will talk of getting you out."

He understood. He thanked me and walked away, weighted down by hopelessness and bad nature. I watched him through the gate. A drab old man in old worn clothes wandering from puddle to puddle of yellow light. It was as though he was the spirit of China, now broken and leaving me. Leaving me forever, for I could tell he would not outlive my father. If his wife did, I swore I would take care of her.

My father's China no longer exists except in him and in other men who try to live true to the dream of China in their hearts. Perhaps like the heaven of Christian converts it is theirs both as an ideal to strive for and a vision of things to come.

I returned to Singapore alienated from the China I saw, but no less eager to listen to my father's stories of the most beautiful of beautiful lands. A country is only as good as its men. My father is a good man . . . whichever country can claim him as its own.

Singapore is very separate from China.

123

The Lady in Red

Felix Chia

Sometime back in the halcyon days when the calypso and rhumba-loving West Indians danced under the moonlight, Hollywood blared the hit of the day, a catchy rhumba called "The Lady in Red." But as far as the three men who had just walked down the gangway of a luxury cruiser were concerned, their spirits were far from the happy notes of the merrymakers singing the opening lines of that song: "Oh, the lady in red, the fellas are crazy of the lady in red! . . ."

The three men seemed to be lost in deep thought. They looked worried and were silent as they made their way down with the many other passengers. They even appeared to reveal a shadow of fear, if one scrutinized them closely! But what was there to fear, especially when they had just returned from a pleasure cruise, one might ask rightly. The short holiday must have been a merry one, judging from the jovial mood of the other passengers. Did they not enjoy the trip? And if they did not, they would surely display only disappointment, and not guilt or fear.

One of the three gentlemen, whom I should introduce simply as "the gentleman"—short for gentleman-at-large, for he was indeed just that—seemed the most worried and frightened of the trio. And although all three were craning their necks and straining their eyes at the passengers around the gangway, as though looking among the crowd for some mysterious person, the gentleman was the most desperate of all.

The gentleman, although engrossed deeply in his searching, could not help thinking about the trip all three had taken together during the past few days. His mind went back to the evening when they boarded the ship, all set for a merry time . . .

125

The final siren hastening visitors to leave the *S.S. Terang Bulan* rang through the air. Scores of people hastened down the gangway, leaving behind those whom they had wished a fond farewell and a happy holiday. The pleasure boat then steamed out of the harbour and the five-hundred-odd passengers were all set for a good time on board the floating hotel that was to roam the sea aimlessly for the next few days.

"Now—here, here we come!" said a man leaning against the ship's railing, and the waves rocked gently by as the ship sailed out into the open sea. "Wonder where this place is?" asked another man who stood next to him. "My map tells me that it's a tiny paradise isle somewhere near the Christmas Island. A lovely island with beautiful scenery, no volcanoes, plenty of sunshine, and lovely native girls who sing and dance all day and night!" said yet another man who was with the other two. "I can't wait to get there!" said the first. "Neither can I!" joined in the second. "And I wish I was already there!" interjected the last of the three men. They laughed and made their way to the bar.

The trio were good friends. They had each paid a handsome sum for the cabin suites they had booked for the cruise, each valuing their privacy more than their money! Besides being able to afford the expensive fare, there was also their uncomfortable feeling that, being full-blooded men, it was impossible to sleep with other men. The man who had spoken first was a wealthy remiser, the second speaker was a successful property broker, and the last of the three, as mentioned earlier, was a gentleman-at-large. Friends called him that because he never answered when asked what he did for a living. They knew that he had recently inherited a large portion of his grandfather's fortune. And he and the property broker had also just made some money at the stock exchange with the tips their remiser friend had given them. They were now giving their tipper a treat on this trip.

Like all bar-flies the three men—all in their thirties—sat on the high stools at the counter. They had just ordered a bottle of their favourite whisky, and had just finished their first drink, when a sweet, cooing voice over the loudspeakers invited them all to dinner. "Please keep this for us, Ah Koh. We'll be back soon," said the remiser, pointing at their bottle. They then left for the dining saloon.

The three friends were men of fancy, and the bond that fostered their association was the common ideal all shared—their partiality for the three "W's," which stood for whimsy, wine, and women. The noise and the smoke from the casino which had just opened attracted their attention. They had finished dinner and took their seats in front of the dealer at the Blackjack table. Her smooth hands flipped and slid the cards deftly with ease and confidence. "Twenty-one! I wish I had staked more!" said the gentleman boisterously. "Take it easy, sir. We have a limit here. We're not real gamblers. We want everyone to have a bit of fun. We don't want anyone to jump overboard because he has no more money in the world!" said the smiling female croupier with an Australian accent.

The trio played for nearly two hours. They could not keep their eyes away from the croupier. They stared at her low-cut dress. She kept tugging up her shoulder straps because her cleavage protruded too much for her liking. The three friends kept on looking and kept on winning. She continued to pull up her straps and the dealer kept losing out to the trio.

"Gentlemen, the cards are on the table," said the Australian woman with a smile as she twitched her eyebrows in the direction of the table's green surface. "That's true. But it's so boring to look at the cards being shuffled, cut, and dealt. And looking elsewhere relieves our eyes of the strain of reading cards, once they are dealt. It also lets us relax for a pleasant moment or two!" replied the gentleman, looking at her with a gleam in his eyes. "But you can look elsewhere," she countered, still smiling. "Ah! But there are not such pretty sights elsewhere!" joined in the remiser. "Unless you consider the empty deck in front of us beautiful to look at!" The three friends laughed, and so too did the other four players who flanked the trio.

One of these players, a man of fifty or so, balding and bespectacled, sat at the end of the table, where the blonde Australian girl stood facing the players. She had been endowed with a lovely and large figure, larger than most of the apples that come from her country! The man with the glasses had been concentrating on his game, but he had also been throwing sheepish glances in the direction of the girl. And when he heard the piece of conversation that had just taken place, and had seen how sportingly she had taken the quips lashed at her, he became braver: taking off his glasses and cleaning them with his handkerchief, he stared at her fully in the face. And then his eyes roved to that same spot the three friends had been eyeing all this while. "Oh no, not you too, sir. You must be a Johnny-come-lately!" she quipped, with an even bigger smile. The man put on his spectacles and picked up his cards in embarrassment, trying hard to look serious. "Never too late to start!" said the property broker from the centre of the table. The crowd and the croupier laughed. The man with the glasses looked down at his cards.

The dealer, a local girl, changed places with the croupier, and after three deals the croupier-turned-dealer managed to win back some of the chips from the three friends. The remiser stood up and said, "Our luck's running out. Let's quit. Here's something for bringing us luck," and he handed the dealer a few chips worth about fifty dollars. She smiled broadly and cooed, "Thank you, sir. Come again tomorrow evening and have some fun!"

"Sure, but what kind of fun?" asked the remiser.

"The kind you had just now!" she replied.

"Er . . . Yes, okay. We'll be here," he said. He wanted to say more but thought the better of it.

"For bringing us bad luck, you mean! We were winning and enjoying ourselves until she changed our luck," said the gentleman. "You know how it is . . . beautiful things can be deadly!" said the property broker. "It's only a bait. Who knows, I might have luck inviting her for a drink when she's off duty! The start of something big? There's a few evenings to go yet. We've just begun the trip," laughed the remiser. They headed for the bar.

They were lucky. They had won some hundreds of dollars among them. "This," said the gentleman gleefully, holding a handful of fifties and twenties, "should give me back the four hundred dollars I spent on that bottle of 'Chateau Quickpiss' at the Utopia Hotel last week!" When they had drunk the bottle they had asked the bartender to hold for them, they ordered another. They drank heartily and soon were in high spirits. "Shall we?" asked the gentleman.

"Of course! I hope it's a good show," replied the property broker. The remiser smiled and said, "What are we waiting for?" and led the way to the upper deck where an X-rated movie was about to be shown; and in his mind were thoughts of the croupier! It was midnight.

The gentleman was the first to rise the next morning. He knocked at the cabins of his two friends, and they all found their way to breakfast. "Let's have a swim after this," suggested the gentleman while munching on his crackers. "In that fish tank?" asked the remiser. "Something's better than nothing," replied the gentleman. "He's right. Come on," coaxed the property broker. They went to their cabins, changed into swim shorts, and headed for the pool.

"It's like having a hot bath. The water's too hot!" said the gentleman. "Never mind. Look there. Not bad . . ." remarked the remiser. "Not quite standard equipment. They're a trifle too small!" said the property broker. "How big do you like them? She's no Dolly Parton but she could be jolly!" the gentleman said, looking at a particular woman in a bikini, one among the other few who were frolicking at the other end of the pool. "Wonder who they are. Don't their men swim? Or are they without men?" asked the property broker. "I hope so!" said the remiser.

"Hope for what?" asked the gentleman.

"That they're without men!" replied the remiser.

"Why don't we find out?" asked the property broker.

"Why not? Let's." said the other two. They swam toward the other end of the pool, and halfway across, four men jumped in and splashed water playfully on the faces of the bikini-clad women. These four men also dashed the hopes of the three friends. "You win some, you lose some! Let's have a drink and listen to the band. Probably get a chance to dance too!" said the gentleman.

"Lead the way and get a bottle from the bar," said the property broker to the remiser. "Okay," replied the remiser.

The other two went to the dance hall. The orchestra was playing a selection of old tunes, the sweet and sentimental songs of yesteryear. The three friends sat down near the band and began to drink as soon as the remiser came with a waiter who brought along a bottle, a jug full of ice, and water. They gave the waiter a fat tip. "Why do they still play songs meant for old fogies? I wish they'd play our kind of music," said the remiser. "Send in requests," suggested the property broker. The remiser went up to the platform and whispered into a musician's ear.

There was a big crowd dancing on the floor while others filled the tables, watching, drinking, and listening to the music. The dance hall was soon packed to capacity. The roving eyes of the three friends suddenly focussed on the same object. They liked what they saw. She was young, fair of complexion, with long, wavy hair; she wore a sleeveless, flaming red dress and sat a few tables away from them. She was alone.

"If you're thinking what I'm thinking, I think you'd better wait a while," said the gentleman with a smile. "I'm thinking what you're thinking, and I too think that we ought to be a little patient," replied the remiser.

"Very well. Let's warm our seats a little longer," said the property broker. The music played on, the dancers danced, and the three friends continued to look in the direction of the lady in red.

"What a gorgeous pair of 'Bo Derek' she's got! Look at the unblemished skin, the starry eyes, the high nose, and those sensuous lips. And her tresses!" thought the property broker to himself. He was not alone in these thoughts. None of the three spoke. They watched her in frustrating silence. Their blissful dreams came to a sudden end when the lady in red got up from her seat and walked briskly away! "We waited too long this time!" said the property broker. They laughed and went to answer the call for lunch. "Why worry? Tomorrow's another day!" said the gentleman.

They ate in silence but their eyes roved from table to table. Although the saloon was large, they could tell plainly that the lady in red was nowhere in sight. "Could she be dieting and have gone to the coffee shop for a small sandwich? Or was she lunching from a tray in her cabin?" the property broker asked himself. And as if reading each others' minds, they ate slowly to make certain that they would be the last to leave the dining saloon. She could come for a late lunch, all three thought to themselves. They finally left when the gong sounded that lunch was over. They headed for the bar, with a faint hope of seeing her there.

"The bird has flown!" said the remiser as he sipped his drink. "There's a chance, however, that she may be at the bingo session at three-thirty," said the property broker. The gentleman smiled and said, "Very optimistic!" The property broker replied with a grin, "Will you count yourself out if I'm right?"

"Why?" the gentleman asked as he poured himself another drink.

"For doubting me!" said the property broker. "Will you scratch on the course if she's not there, and drop out of the chase if we see her again later?" asked the gentleman. "Even odds! But the prize is too great to risk being disqualified from the hunt. I shall pass and take my chances against you!" replied the property broker. The remiser raised his glass and toasted: "To the victor goes the first opportunity to taste the spoils!" In the typical fashion of the three friends, they had agreed to share among themselves whatever fun and games they could get, as they had been doing all along, no matter who found the prize first. "Remember. We must toss for second place after the winner has had his conquest. If we can find her that is!" said the gentleman.

"Number one!" bawled a low, loud voice from the loudspeakers at the dance hall, where the bingo session was held. The sound of muffled, clicking wood was heard, and as the announcer pulled another token from the pouch, he called out, "Two's company!" "Three's a crowd!" followed the next token. A stifled gasp filled the air. "What an interesting set of numbers to open the first game!" exclaimed the property broker. "Will the next one be a 'four' I wonder?"

The property broker's curiosity was satisfied when the number "four" indeed was next. "Amazing. Are they rigging the game?" asked the remiser. "Someone must win!" said the gentleman. "It could be fixed for their accomplices to win all the games!" replied the remiser. "Don't joke!" said the property broker.

"But I am joking!" laughed the remiser. The sequence broke at the fifth number when the number thirty-seven was called out. All this while the three pairs of eyes roved about the dance hall. They saw a lady in red but it wasn't the one they were looking for. They were disappointed, and did not pay much attention to the game.

Luck held with the three friends. "Bingo!" cried out the property broker when the fourth game was played. Three games later the remiser won. It was the jackpot prize and he said gleefully, "There's enough winnings here to drink ourselves silly. What are we waiting for? She's not here. Where in hell is she?"

"That's probably just where she is!" said the property broker. They cashed their winning coupons and went to the bar.

"What shall we do to find her?" asked the gentleman. They continued to drink, and the more they drank, the more they thought of her. "I'm sick of stretching my neck whenever I see red!" said the remiser. "But good things are hard to find," said the gentleman. They spent their time at the bar until it was dinner time. By then they had all drunk too much. They staggered to the dining saloon, ate little,

131

and, feeling that they were about to pass out, made their way to the cabins and slept.

The next morning the three friends were at the breakfast table, looking none the worse for the many drinks they had had the night before. "I'm sure she's somewhere around, unless she's a kind of 'blithe spirit'!" said the gentleman. They were still determined to find the lady in red. Nothing else had been in their minds since they first saw her. "I wonder if she's seasick and having a terrible time in bed," said the remiser. "How could she? She looked all right to me," said the property broker. "Perhaps we should ask around for her." "No, not that! What reason have we got to pry into her whereabouts? Who do we look for? A lady in red? You just don't do these things!" said the remiser.

The trio spent a rather dull day, drinking and pulling the arms of the jackpot machines. By four in the afternoon, the gentleman felt bored and had gone to sleep. The property broker had gone to see the fishing contest held at the ship's stern, when they were anchored somewhere off the coast of Pulau Tioman. He enjoyed himself when someone allowed him to take a hand or two at trying to get a bite. He caught a fish but it was far smaller than the size that would have won him the prize of $200—which the captain offered. He felt a little tired. He had been looking around hard in case the lady in red was somewhere among the crowd. She was not. And he too went off to take a nap. Only the remiser remained with the jackpot machines, and played until he had lost $250. He went to the bar and drank alone. He stayed there until dinner time.

Once again the trio sat down for dinner with roving eyes. They refused to give up the hunt for the lady in red. "I've got an excellent idea," said the gentleman. "Why don't we look for her separately? Let's play a kind of 'treasure hunt.' To the finder goes the privilege of you-know-what! But we must pledge that after he has succeeded, the finder must tell the other two her cabin number. Allow the other two to have a chance, and as I have suggested we must toss to see who goes next. Okay?"

"That's a brilliant idea. But why did it take so long to think of it?" asked the remiser.

"My friend. Desperation rattles the imagination and makes it work harder!" replied the gentleman. "What happens if two of us or all of us meet up with her at the same time?" asked the property broker. "Then again, my friends, let us indulge in the childish tossing of *cham cham pah!*" laughed the gentleman. "Let's begin the search right after dinner," said the remiser enthusiastically. "Why waste time? What better time is there than right now?" asked the property broker. The gentleman smiled and drank his glass of water. Rising from his chair, he said, "Gentlemen, let the hunt begin!" And the trio left the dining room to go their separate ways.

The remiser chose to look around deck 2. The bow of deck 1 was the starting point for the gentleman, and the property broker began his search from the stern of deck 1. The latter pair were to meet halfway, and then one of them would go upstairs to bring the remiser to come down to the lower deck to continue the search. From then on, each was entitled to track their quarry at random; they would meet at the bar at a certain time, with or without the lady in red. Deck 3, housing only a coffee shop, could be visited by any one of them whenever they felt so inclined.

It seemed an excellent arrangement, but the three friends had overlooked an important possibility. What if the finder found it difficult to part from the lady in red, once captivated by her charms? After all, they could be hunting for several hours. Over-zealousness was perhaps the cause of that little bit of muddled thinking. Or perhaps each of them had something up his sleeve?

The gallivanting trio began their search in earnest. They strolled along the passageways of the cabins, they popped their heads into the coffee house and the massage salon, they even screened all those seated in the dance hall and those dancing on the floor. They were quite thorough. The tables of the casino, the corridors of jackpot machines, the restaurant, the nooks and corners of the open decks, and the swimming pool were sieved by the eager three friends, as the ship continued to cruise along the calm sea. Everyone was having a good time, and the trio were expecting a much better time if only they could find the lady in red.

The minutes ticked by, and soon an hour had passed. The three friends had still not found their lady in red. Another fruitless hour passed. During these two hours they each visited the bar intermittently in hope of seeing her there, and if not, of meeting one another to commiserate. Strangely enough, they repeatedly missed one another at the bar. They were about to give up the ghost!

It was a little before midnight. The remiser sat brooding at one of the three small tables in the corner of the bar. He was alone. He had drunk a half bottle of whisky in the past twenty minutes! He appeared anxious, even frightened. And, despite the air-conditioning, beads of perspiration dotted his forehead. He drank up the contents of his glass and poured himself another drink. "Wonder where the two are!" he muttered to himself. He did not have long to wait. The property broker appeared in front of him a few moments later, at first quite unaware of the remiser's presence. The property broker sat down and poured himself a drink—two empty glasses had been put on the table by the remiser.

Uncorking the bottle with one hand and filling the glass with ice from the jug nearby with the other, the property broker asked, "Have you been here long?" He seemed disgusted. The exuberance he had shown all along had disappeared. He looked glum, and words came out of his mouth only with great difficulty. Strangely, too, the remiser was just as quiet. It was as if both had lost their tongues! The two drank in silence, and the property broker's question remained unanswered. He did not bother to repeat it.

The whisky had been drunk, and that included a half bottle the property broker had ordered when the first bottle was empty. It was now one in the morning. Both gave out a yawn, and the remiser threw his head sideways into the air, indicating that he had had enough for the day—enough of everything! His friend responded with a shrug of the shoulders as though to ask: "What else is there to do?" and rose to follow the remiser out of the bar. They made their way to their cabins in awkward silence. The remiser still looked anxious and frightened, and the property broker appeared just as irritated as before. They closed their cabin doors with a soft exchange of "Goodnight!"

The lights along the cabin corridor burned brightly. All was quiet but for the splashing of gentle waves washing against the sides of the ship. It was about two-thirty in the morning. "I doubt if they're still there. The bar is closed by now. I'll apologise to them tomorrow," said the gentleman to himself, as he walked along the corridor to his cabin. He unlocked his door quietly and went inside, wishing that his friends had not gone to bed. He was exuberant, and was even whistling a tune as he changed into his pyjamas. He thought of waking up his friends but feared that they would be

134

annoyed twice over—by waiting in vain for him at the bar, and then being woken at a late hour. So the gentleman went to bed and slept soundly.

The gentleman woke up the next morning, still bright and cheerful. He knocked at his friends' cabins but got no response. His watch showed that it was a quarter to ten. He hastened to the dining saloon. His friends were not there, and he sat down for breakfast. When he had eaten, he searched for them. "So there you are!" he said when he saw them sitting in deck chairs. He pulled up a chair and sat next to them. "Look, I know you're mad at me. I'm sorry that I didn't go to the bar last night. I wasn't through till about two-thirty and I was sure that you two would have given up waiting for me. Hey! I'm really sorry. Don't be childish. Why are you both so glum and silent?" The two friends continued to ignore him. He smiled and shook his head in disbelief, and said, "Come on, boys! Never mind. Let me tell you what happened last night. I found her in the most unlikely place. Well . . ." but before he could continue, the remiser interrupted, "Please, I don't want to talk about last night. Let's imagine that last night never happened!" The look of anxiety and fear was still there in his eyes. And with the same tone of disgust, the property broker said, "I want to forget about last night too!"

"Well," sighed the gentleman. "I refuse to believe what is happening, but I won't talk about it. How about a swim?" The two friends shook their heads in disagreement. "I prefer to enjoy the breeze here," said the property broker. The remiser closed his eyes as he reclined, his hands supporting his head. "We still have two days and nights to go. It's too long a time for us to act like dumb creatures," said the gentleman. "What about a beer then?" The property broker nudged the remiser, who opened his eyes and said, "No thanks. I want to take a nap. I hardly slept a wink last night, or rather this morning!" The other two friends then left for the bar. They drank their beer with great satisfaction.

"What's wrong with him?" asked the gentleman. "And you too, you look pretty mad! Why?" The property broker puffed at his cigarette and said, "He seems too frightened to talk. I think he's in some kind of shock! I tried hard last night to get him to speak up but he kept his mouth shut as tight as a clam. And I was embarrassed, too, about my own encounter with the damn so-called 'lady in red'! But I now feel that I'll be better off after I've got it off my chest!"

"That's more like it! Have another beer and start at the beginning. I'll do the same, and after that we could try to straighten out our good friend," said the gentleman. And soon the two friends were talking in earnest, just as they'd always done . . .

The morning sun shone on the remiser's face. His closed eyelids flickered and he stirred to move his deck chair a little away, behind where the shadows fell. He wished he had brought his sunglasses along—the sun was too pleasantly warm to retreat from. He had tried to get a nap but there were too many thoughts in his mind—frightening and disturbing memories of the night before! The remiser was now a suppressed nervous wreck. He did not want his friends to know of his terror—but he knew that they were too perceptive to be misled. The truth was that he had become convulsive with fear as soon as he had entered his cabin the night before, after the property broker had gone into his own cabin. He had tucked himself under the blanket and had tried to sleep off the beginning of the new day, but with little success!

His nightmare lingered in his mind. He could still see plainly that vivid and terrifying sight, just at the moment when ecstasy was within his hungry grasp. And then his frantic, headlong flight, escaping from the apparition. He wished he had accepted the gentleman's offer to the drinks. It would do him good. So he rose from the deck chair and walked into the bar to join his friends.

Meanwhile the property broker and the gentleman were talking excitedly, and the tone of their conversation was nearly argumentative. "I can understand how disgusted you must have felt. But I still say you must have been mistaken. Damn it! I should know!" said the gentleman.

"Hell! I too should know!" retorted the property broker. "For the last time," said the gentleman, "all I know is that I met her at the coffee shop while the midnight show was going on. It took me only a few minutes to spot her in the shadows. There she was—in the same red dress. I sat down a few seats away from her. Suddenly I moved to sit next to her under the pretext that I could not get a clear view of the screen. The rest was basic: an accidental touch of her hand, a smile and an apology, and I was on home ground!"

"And you had a fine time with her?" asked the property broker.

"Yes I did! She was beautiful, she was fair, and she was game! I can still feel the throbbing of those firm roses on her chest. The aroma of her lovely body is still in my nostrils. I must see her again—now! And, my good friend, she was a real woman, in every sense! Please don't try to tell me otherwise!" said the gentleman with conviction.

With equally great faith in his own experience, the property broker answered, "Something's wrong. I met her about 11:00 or so. The dance hall was packed. There was some silly kind of dance competition going on. I had to stand behind seven or eight lines of people. I was exasperated. I could hardly get a view of the front. I was about to leave when I saw her, all alone in a tight corner. Her red dress and her fair skin glowed in the dark. 'Luck,' I muttered to myself and walked toward her. I smiled and she smiled back. And that was all it needed! I asked her if she would like a drink. She shook her head but took my arm and ushered me outside.

"We went to the swimming pool area. It was deserted. She seemed to know where to bring me, just like a true professional. She was, as we all know, very beautiful, and she turned out to be obliging and inviting. I chose to whet my appetite first before suggesting that we go to bed, and I kissed her and fondled her 'Matterhorn' with a passion I've never known before! But when I touched her down below, I was aghast! An inch or so of soft flesh greeted my fingers as I ran them down her belly. Now you know why I'm so disgusted. It's never happened to me before. I'm so sick with shame to have kissed a man like that. And when 'she' asked me what was wrong when I withdrew my hand and pushed 'her' away, the husky voice I heard turned my guts inside out!" the property broker concluded with a deep sigh.

"I find it difficult to believe you . . ." said the gentleman, but the property broker interrupted: "But I'm not a liar!" The gentleman looked at his friend appealingly and continued, "I'm not calling you one. But it just does not make sense. Surely I know that I had a good time with a woman last night!"

"And I also know that I nearly slept with an *Ah Kua* last night!" replied the property broker emphatically.

The gentleman looked puzzled, and so too did his good friend. "I guess it's no use arguing. Let's find out from our friend what's bothering him. Make him talk at all costs. It'll be interesting to hear what he has to say," said the gentleman. "We'll do that. Let's go and find him," said the property broker. It was at that point that the remiser appeared at the bar. With a smile the gentleman beckoned him to sit down. He sat and they ordered him a beer. Despite the coaxing of his two friends to make him tell them his story, it was only after he had drunk a few pints before he was able to begin.

Nervously, he said, "It was in the casino that I met her. I went from table to table. Suddenly I saw her sitting all alone, not far from the roulette table. Of course it was her flowing hair and red dress that caught my eye. I rubbed my hands in glee. I went up to her and asked if she would like to try her luck at the table at my expense. She shook her head. 'I see that you are alone. Shall we take a stroll on the deck? The fresh air will be good for us,' I said. She smiled and rose from her chair, took my arm, and off we went all the way up the steps.

"There was no one around and we walked till we reached the bow. In the shadows of the open area under the upper deck, she smiled at me and her eyes encouraged me to make love to her. I kissed her fully on the lips. She returned my kisses with equal sensation. She ran her hands all over my body. I reciprocated with all my energy! We worked ourselves up in a cosy corner, and the thought of a comfortable cool bed became more and more inviting as we made love. I'd bring her to my cabin if she'd agree, I thought. And all I knew was that I must have her. Nothing else mattered, not even tomorrow! If it was a question of money, I was prepared to give her whatever she wanted. I was in ecstasy!"

The remiser stopped to gulp down a mouthful of beer. "Yes, yes. What happened?" asked the impatient property broker. "Tell us. The suspense is killing me!" The remiser drew a deep breath and downed the remainder of his beer. He said, "You will not believe me. It's too absurd to believe . . ."

"For goodness sake! Tell us and we'll decide whether to believe you or not!" said the property broker. "Okay. Everything went fine until I asked her to follow me to my cabin. I held her hand and walked ahead, then all of a sudden a cold wind seemed to blow through my body and then I heard a soft, shrill cackle followed by a high-pitched scream. I turned around and my God! The once desirable woman we all had been coveting has turned into an old hag with long teeth. Her eyes were bloodshot and she was trying to embrace me. I pushed her aside and ran all the way to the bar. It was about 10:30 and I sat there drinking until you came," concluded the remiser, looking at the property broker.

"Well, friends, I was the second one to encounter her," the property broker said. "But I was more fortunate because she preferred to become an *Ah Kua* for me, instead of that horrible creature she became for you!" The gentleman smiled. Why, he thought, surely he knew best. "Gentlemen! I have nothing to say except that I want you to follow me to her cabin, where I slept with her. It will also allow me to fulfill my part of the bargain—to introduce you both to her!" The remiser fidgetted and the property broker looked away. "Come on, now . . . it's broad daylight!" said the gentleman as he touched the shoulders of his two friends and made them rise. The trio went out of the bar, the gentleman walking in between the other two, his hands still on their shoulders.

The gentleman knew exactly where to go. "This is it!" he said when he stopped at the last cabin in the corridor. The property broker was curious. Fear crept into the remiser's face. The gentleman, confident and smiling, knocked at the door. They stood there for a few minutes as he knocked repeatedly. The door remained shut. The three friends walked away. "She could be out, somewhere in the ship. Let's try and find her again!" said the gentleman.

The gentleman led the way, going from place to place, covering almost every inch of the ship. The property broker followed him with a sense of nausea and the remiser with a sense of fear! When at last even the gentleman had given up hope of finding the lady in red, they agreed to ask the captain about the cabin which had not responded to their knocks. "But gentlemen," said the grey-haired captain. "Cabin 400 is unoccupied. It's been locked and barred from occupancy for a long time now. I'm not even sure why." "Thank you, sir. You've been most helpful in settling a small dispute among us three," said the property broker. The captain smiled and the three left for the bar.

There, the wall of silence once more erected itself; the trio drank quietly. This time, however, the silence enveloped the gentleman as well. Could he have been mistaken? Was it not the cabin next to it or the one opposite that he had entered? Or even indeed was the cabin on a different deck? Much as he wished he could believe it, he realized that his memory was far too good to forget this detail. He had only had one drink at dinner that night, and had stayed sober throughout the evening, because he knew he would have to be clear-headed to pursue his prey. Also, after such an enthralling experience, how could he forget where to find her again!

The three friends, who had been so lively and talkative when they boarded the ship, were now a silent trio of confused men! Their last day on the ship was spent in casual but moody conversation, as their eyes worked harder than their tongues. They hoped to see the lady in red again, even just once more.

Just before dinner-time, when his friends were on their way to the dining saloon, the gentleman, unsatisfied with this seemingly impossible situation which contradicted his own experience, looked hard at the linen on his bed. Could it all have been a wet dream? And wouldn't such a realistic dream have left tell-tale marks on the bedsheet? But the maid had already changed the bedsheets, so he couldn't examine the ones he'd slept in last night.

The gentleman's annoyance turned into fear when he accepted finally that the lady in red was a ghost or a kind of *pontianak*. And his fear became sharper when he wondered why it had chosen to frighten the remiser, ridicule the property broker, and make love to him as a beautiful woman! His flesh roughened with goose pimples during that last night on the ship. And by arrangement, unknown to the property broker, the gentleman slept with the remiser in the latter's cabin that night, much to the remiser's delight. Some men do sleep with men after all!

Notes on the Authors

Gopal Baratham, a neurosurgeon by profession, has published two collections of short stories, *Figments of Experience* (1981) and *People Make You Cry* (1988), as well as two novels, *Sayang* and *A Candle or the Sun*, both published in 1991. Dr. Baratham was given the Southeast Asian Write Award in 1991.

Felix Chia is best known for his two books about the Singaporean Baba/Nonya community and for his plays in the Baba dialect. *The Babas* (1980) was followed by *Ala Sayang!* (1983), and the two plays *Pileh Menantu* (1984) and *Laki Tua Beni Muda* (1985). *The Lady in Red* (1984) is a book of short stories, while *Reminiscences* (also 1984) is autobiographical.

Rebecca Chua is the author of a book of stories, *The Newspaper Editor and Other Stories* (1981).

Ho Minfong has published three novels, *Sing to the Dawn* (1975), *Rice Without Rain* (1986), and *Clay Marble* (1991), as well as numerous short stories.

Ho Poh Fun has published numerous short stories and poems, and now teaches at Raffles Junior College in Singapore.

Shirley Lim won the Commonwealth Poetry Prize in 1980 for her first collection of poems, *Crossing the Peninsula and Other Poems*. *Another Country*, a book of stories, appeared in 1982. Since then, she has published two further collections of poems, *No Man's Grove*

(1985) and *Modern Secrets: New and Selected Poems* (1989). She has also published and edited books of criticism.

The late *Lim Thean Soo* (1924-1991) wrote poems, plays, short stories, and novels but he is best known for his fiction. The short stories are collected in *Fourteen Short Stories* (1979), *Bits of Paper and Other Stories* (1980), *The Parting Gift and Other Stories* (1981), *Blues and Carnations* (1985), and *Eleven Bizarre Tales* (1990). His novels include *Destination Singapore* (1976), *Ricky Star* (1978), *The Towkay of Produce Street* (1991), and *Singaporama* (1991).

The late *Gregory Nalpon* has published one story, "The Rose and the Silver Key," in *Singapore Short Stories* (1989), edited by Robert Yeo.

Kirpal Singh, senior lecturer in the Nanyang Technological University in Singapore, has published two books of poems, *Twenty Poems* (1977) and *Palm Readings* (1986). He has also published numerous critical pieces, edited several volumes of criticism, and is preparing a book of short stories. He is also a science fiction buff.

Woo Keng Thye, a renal specialist at the Singapore General Hospital, has written short stories and novels. The stories are collected in *A Question of Time* (1983) and *Encounter and Other Stories* (1989). Dr. Woo has published two novels, *Web of Tradition* (1986) and *Winds of Change* (1991).

Robert Yeo, the editor of this volume, is senior lecturer in the Nanyang Technological University in Singapore. He has published three books of poetry, a novel, and seen four of his plays produced. Among the prominent titles are *And Napalm Does Not Help* (poems, 1977); *The Adventures of Holden Heng* (novel, 1986); and *One Year Back Home* (play, 1990). He has also edited numerous anthologies of short stories and plays.

Ovidia Yu has written many plays, stories, and a novel. Among the plays performed by leading theatre companies in Singapore are *Dead on Cue* (1987), *Round and Round the Dining Table* (1988), and *Three Fat Virgins Unassembled* (1992). A novel, *Miss Moorthy Investigates*, was published in 1989.

Glossary

ada baik?: "How are you?" A Malay greeting which literally means "Are you OK?"

ada nasib: "I am lucky." Of Malay origin.

Ah Kua: a transvestite.

ASEAN: The Association of Southeast Asian Nations, a political and economic alliance comprising Indonesia, Brunei, Singapore, Malaysia, the Philippines, and Thailand.

attap: Dried palm leaves used as roofing in a traditional Malay house.

baju kurong: A long Malay dress worn over a sarong.

bedak sejok: A cosmetic face powder.

bee hoon: Rice vermicelli, usually stir-fried with other ingredients.

blachan: Prawn paste.

cham cham pah: A children's game.

chingay: A Chinese celebration occurring on the 22nd day after the Chinese New Year, often featuring men walking on tall stilts.

intan: A diamond-like gem.

kampong: A small village.

kebaya: The top part of a woman's dress, traditionally worn with a *sarong,* a piece of cloth wrapped around the waist.

Kempeitai: The Japanese secret police during the Second World War, used to subjugate Japanese-occupied territory.

laksa: A noodle dish with spicy soup.

lallang: Tall, sharp grass; a tropical weed.

lidi: The vein of a palm leaf.

Mari-lah: "Come, let's go." Malay in origin.

Masok: "Come in." Malay in origin.

mee siam: A spicy noodle dish.

namaskharam: A traditional Indian farewell gesture, with upright palms together accompanied by a bow.

nasib: Luck.

padi: A rice field.

pandan: A plant with aromatic leaves used to wrap cakes.

pontianak: A vampire. Malay in origin.

popia: A spring roll.

pulau: An island.

pulut: Unpolished rice.

sinseh: A traditional Chinese physician.

tongkang: A bumboat.